W9-CEY-688

January 6th 1996

Dear Miss Woolford:

I appreciate so much your letter and the wonderful photographs. I assume you want them back; perhaps I could have some of them copied, first?

I hope to take some photographs of the house and the neighborhood as it is now to send to you. There have been enormous changes in both. Most striking: the house is now hemmed in by other houses. I had no idea it was once in the midst of fields!

The early deeds indicate that there was some structure on this site from about 1880. Do you think your parents bought something very small and added the studio--that is clear from the photographs--as well as some of the other rooms? I would be most interested to know what you think.

I am a writer, like your parents, but a novelist and playwright; my most recent book is called "Matron of Honor." I am enclosing a copy. I bought the house from a painter called Jerry Cajko--his paint is all over the studio floor--and he is the one who claimed the house was 200 years old. Before that it belonged to a sculptor who left an anteater in the garden (Jerry took it.)

It's so interesting to learn that you parents were friends with the artists of their day--I imagine your collection is unique.

With best wishes,

For Polk Woolford –
with happy memories of
716 Acequia Madre

Sallie Bingham
Santa Fe
January, 1996

Matron
of Honor

BOOKS BY
SALLIE BINGHAM

Small Victories

Upstate

Passion and Prejudice

The Way It Is Now

The Touching Hand

After Such Knowledge

Sallie Bingham

Matron of Honor

ZOLAND BOOKS
Cambridge, Massachusetts

For my sister

Copyright © Sallie Bingham

All rights reserved. No part of this book may be used or
reproduced in any manner whatsoever without written
permission, except in the case of brief quotations
embodied in critical articles and reviews.

FIRST EDITION

10 9 8 7 6 5 4 3 2

Text design by Boskydell Studio
Printed in the United States of America

This book is printed on acid-free paper,
and its binding materials have been
chosen for strength and durability.

Library of Congress Cataloging-in-Publication Data
Bingham, Sallie.
Matron of honor / Sallie Bingham. —1st ed.
p. cm.
ISBN 0-944072-38-0 (acid-free paper)
1. Upper classes—Southern States—Fiction. 2. Marriage—Southern
States—Fiction. 3. Sisters—Southern States—Fiction. 4. Women—
Southern States—Fiction. I. Title.
PS3552.I5M38 1994
813'.54—dc20   93-33845
CIP

Matron of Honor

CHAPTER ONE

*T*HE YELLOW-AND-WHITE-striped canvas tent that would hold five hundred people at a pinch arrived the morning of the day before the wedding, folded in stiff layers in Harvey's flatbed truck. Mrs. Mason, who had been in her garden since six, heard the truck coming up the hill and went to meet it. She stopped at the garden entrance, placing one hand on the limestone pedestal from which a cast-iron cupid, weighing several hundred pounds, had been ripped by thieves.

Harvey stopped his truck when he saw her. "Wanted to get the tent up before the heat," he said. He was a florid man who did all the hauling for big parties and weddings: setting up hundreds of folding chairs, manhandling stubborn card tables, and pegging down tents in the way least damaging to prized lawns. In the cab beside him, his helpers, Russell and Pete, nodded and smiled at Mrs. Mason.

"I'll meet you over by the house," she said and started along the flagstone path. Her eye ran down the line of moss which had appeared between the flagstones: such a wet spring, the growth was out of hand. I'll have to get to that after the wedding, she thought. She did not care for the shade creatures — moss, fungus, sprawling ivy. Her garden was full of bright perennials that could take any amount of sun.

Mrs. Mason picked up the basket of daisies she had gathered earlier; plain field flowers but prettier than anything at the florist's. Their leaves were folded like narrow hands, already suffering from the heat. Mrs. Mason fought a wish to bury her face in the daisies. She was determined to keep on an even keel; others were depending on her, and a rush at the flowers might bring tears. These were allowed, at the ceremony, for the mother of the bride, but not before. She wondered if other people felt the daily anguish of life as she did, decided they probably did but were good at hiding it, and went up the flagstone path with her basket on her arm.

As she approached her house, Mrs. Mason felt, as always, the fatigued relief of a pilgrim returning from the Holy Land. The trim frame cottage held everything she loved. Beyond the house lay the river, and on the opposite shore, Indiana shimmered in the September sun.

Harvey was waiting for her on the lawn, his belly dropping from his folded arms so that at first she thought he was carrying a checkered sack. "You still want the tent between the magnolias and that path?"

"Run it from the line of the path all the way over to that box hedge, back up against the magnolias; that way people can get to it straight from their cars, if it rains."

"Don't look much like rain," Pete said, squinting at the sky.

"Sure hope it's pretty tomorrow for Miss Apple," Russell chimed in with an unctuousness that irritated Mrs. Mason; she knew he had abandoned a wife and several children on the other side of the river.

"It's supposed to be a lovely day tomorrow," she said, turning away. "You all come in the house at noon and get something to eat. Frankie's frying chicken."

She went in the side door made from logs that had been part of a cabin. They were silvery gray, rough under her hand from long exposure to the sun. The door should have been replaced years ago, but it saddened her to make changes.

Inside, she placed her basket of flowers on the hall floor and crossed to her bedroom. Mr. Mason was sitting on the edge of a chair, finishing his breakfast.

"I've got something to tell you," he said, wiping his mouth.

Mrs. Mason stared at him. Their conversation flowed in loops, in shadowy meanderings, never with abrupt starts or stops.

"What in the world is it?" she asked, looking at the blue china eggcup in the center of his breakfast tray.

"Corinne arrived while you were in the garden." He stood up, dropping his napkin, and came to her. Mrs. Mason was still staring at his eggcup. Then she smelled his crisp cuffs and felt his hands on her shoulders. "Bear up. She wants to see you right away."

Her mind, traveling fast over the responsibilities of the

day, all jumbled now, threatened with confusion, stopped at the thought that at least Harvey did not need her supervision to get the tent up.

Mr. Mason went on, "She told me she rode all night on the Greyhound. I don't know why she didn't fly."

"Where is she?"

"I offered her breakfast but she wouldn't take any. She's terribly afraid she'll be in the way — I mean at the wedding."

"She's staying?"

Mr. Mason smiled at her bewilderment. "Apparently she doesn't want to miss her sister's wedding after all."

"It's too late for her to be matron of honor — she must know that."

"We'll have to see what Apple wants," Mr. Mason said.

Mrs. Mason sighed. "Where is Corinne?"

"In her bedroom."

"I told Frankie to make that room up for the guests." She stopped. "Everything has to change now, doesn't it?"

"Not everything. But we will have to make a place for Corinne. Go on and see her."

"I want to put my daisies in water!"

"I'll take care of your flowers." With one hand, he turned her towards the door.

Mrs. Mason went down the hall on tiptoe. At the door nearest to the stairs, she stopped and studied the wood. Here, where the sun seldom penetrated, the pine had kept its satin sheen. As she lifted her hand to knock, the door opened and she saw her elder daughter.

"Corinne," she said, and kissed her cheek. Then she took a step and put her arms around her daughter. Corinne seemed to shrink, as though her long bones couldn't support even that mild pressure. "You've gotten so thin!" Mrs. Mason cried.

"You always used to say a lady couldn't be too rich or too thin," Corinne said, but the joke fell flat. "I know this is a bad time for me to come home."

Mrs. Mason was staring at her. "What's happened, this time?"

Corinne looked away. The grain of her fair skin seemed to rise like the grain of a piece of wood once it has been stripped with acid.

Mrs. Mason led her into the bedroom. There, in the speckled gloom (Frankie, preparing for guests, had closed the flowered curtains against the heat), she turned her daughter around. She took hold of Corinne's wrist and pressed the sharp bone; she made a dart at her blueberry-colored shirt dress and struck the ledge of her daughter's hipbone. "Why have you come back?"

"Do you really want to know?"

"Yes, I want to know! But first I'm going to ask Frankie to bring us up some coffee."

"I don't want anything," Corinne said.

"Well, I do," Mrs. Mason said, recovering her brightness. She opened the door and called, "Frankie!"

After a minute, she called again, wondering. Frankie never needed to be called twice.

Then they heard her step in the hall. Frankie looked in the door.

5

"Miss Corinne's back," Mrs. Mason said.

"I heard the taxi. Don't you all wake up Miss Apple, she was out till four this morning."

"We won't. Would you bring us some coffee, please? I know you're trying to get the silver done."

"You want an egg?" Frankie asked, coming in the room and looking at Corinne.

"Hello, Frankie. I don't eat eggs," Corinne said.

"I'll fix you some of that rye bread, toasted, with a little butter and Miss Carey's raspberry preserves. You got to eat," Frankie said.

Corinne smiled. Frankie turned away. Her quickness reassured Mrs. Mason; Frankie had the day in hand.

As soon as she was gone, Corinne sat down and put her face on her knees.

"Your father tells me you came all this way on the bus," Mrs. Mason said, sitting down near her.

Corinne said, into her knees, "I left Buddy yesterday, for good. I couldn't bear to ask him for anything, not even money for a plane ticket. I had enough for the bus."

"You were so sensible when you told Apple you weren't well enough to be in the wedding, when you told me you were going to try to possess your heart in patience."

"I'm not so sensible anymore," Corinne said, raising her head. "I tried to stick it out. Last week when we talked, I thought I could stand it at least till the end of the year. But we had a fight yesterday and Buddy slapped my face —" Her voice trembled. "And then Brian called —"

"Not that man," Mrs. Mason said.

"He wanted to talk to me about a problem he's having with his wife."

6

"No, Corinne!"

"I have to listen, Mother."

"Why can't you learn? Please learn," Mrs. Mason pleaded.

"He says he's thinking about a separation."

"How many times —"

Frankie came in with a tray, which she placed on the desk. "We're out of raspberry. I brought you some honey. You like honey," she said.

"Thank you, Frankie," Corinne said.

"Frankie, if you'll answer the phone," Mrs. Mason murmured as Frankie passed her. She nodded, then went out and closed the door smartly.

Mrs. Mason reached for a cup of coffee.

"I love Brian, Mother," Corinne said suddenly, and she slid down onto the floor at her mother's feet.

Mrs. Mason cupped her daughter's head in her hands and kissed her light hair. "Corinne, he's married. He's always going to be married."

"I can't help it," Corinne said, and she knelt against her mother's knees and put her arms around her waist. "I'm in so much pain I can't eat or sleep or work. I just wait to hear from him, wait for him to tell me to come."

Mrs. Mason rocked her daughter. "Why does it go on and on this way?"

"Because of the way he looked at me, that first time, when I was quietly going along with my life. Because of the way he ripped my life —"

"Why should you want your life ripped?"

"Because it was nothing and I didn't even know it."

"Corinne, he'll never marry you, you know that," Mrs. Mason said, close to her daughter's ear.

7

"I know, Mother. I don't care, I just want to be with him."

"You can't be with him, darling. He belongs to somebody else."

"That's why I came home." Corinne sobbed. "I'm trying to get away from him. I had to come home, even in the middle of Apple's wedding."

"That doesn't matter, of all things," Mrs. Mason said, but she knew it did, and even as she was coaxing Corinne to eat a little toast, even as she was breaking it into bits and buttering it for her, she was wondering whether Harvey would remember to put the tent back up against the magnolias.

As soon as she could, Mrs. Mason ran out to check. The tent was lying on the grass in an enormous folded square, and the three men were digging holes for posts. Harvey looked up.

"You won't forget where I want it, will you?" Mrs. Mason asked.

Harvey showed her with his foot exactly where the edge of the tent would be. They separated without speaking another word.

She hurried back to her bedroom, where Mr. Mason was standing in front of the bureau, fastening on his watch.

"I got her to eat some toast," Mrs. Mason said, looking at the beautiful line of his skull through his bright gray hair.

"Child of misfortune." Mr. Mason sighed.

"I felt it when I held her," Mrs. Mason said, going to her husband. "I felt it in her bones — that terrible pliancy."

Mr. Mason put his arms around her. "That gracious pliancy, it might have been — in another time, another place."

"But not in New York City in nineteen seventy."

"No."

"She's left Buddy, she says for good, and she's going back to that awful man."

"I knew it would happen, sooner or later. Buddy's no match for her."

"But not now! I can't give her the attention she deserves!"

"Why is she always in trouble, whereas —"

Their younger daughter came into the room, holding together the waist of the man's pajamas she was wearing. Her hair hung down in a long, raveling braid, and she was barefooted, her toenails painted tangerine. "What have I got to do today? I hope nothing," she said, yawning.

"Your sister's home," Mr. Mason said.

"Cory?" Apple stared at her parents. Then she said, "Oh, good. She can be my matron of honor after all."

"Lila is your matron of honor," Mrs. Mason said.

"I always wanted Cory, I was crushed when she said she couldn't. I only took old Lila as a stopgap."

"Well, it's too late to change now. What would Billy say if you threw out his own sister?"

"He's not that crazy about her. Besides, I want Cory."

"There couldn't possibly be time," Mr. Mason said.

"Time for what?" Apple asked, picking up a Limoges snuffbox and turning it in her fingers.

"Why, for her to feel up to it," her father said.

"And for the dress to be made; Lila's is three sizes too big, even if you could ask her to pass it along," her mother reminded her.

"Frankie can make her dress." Apple dropped the snuffbox

on the puffed seat of her mother's chaise lounge, then picked it up again, like a magpie testing a trinket for her nest. "I like this. Leave it to me in your will."

"The chair or the box?" Mr. Mason asked with an irrepressible smile.

"Both, if possible." Apple grinned at him.

"There's no material for a dress!" Mrs. Mason protested. "All that rust-colored ombré was used."

"Not the piece we bought for Sandra and then she got pregnant," Apple said. "You made me drop her because you said she'd show, but I'm not going to drop Cory. It's my wedding."

"I thought Billy had something to do with it," Mr. Mason said.

"He doesn't care! You think he wants all this fuss?"

"I don't think there really is enough material," Mrs. Mason said.

Mr. Mason grew serious. "Apple, it may not be the best thing for Corinne."

Mrs. Mason added quickly, "And I couldn't possibly ask Frankie, in the middle of all the work she's got to do —"

"I'll ask her," Apple said, and she pressed a button in the wall.

"She's doing the silver!" Mrs. Mason protested.

"I can do the silver, or Cory can," Apple said, and she turned her small face towards her parents and beamed.

"Well, I wash my hands of it," Mr. Mason said. "It seems to me if Frankie can get the dress made in time —" He glanced at his wife and stopped.

Frankie, coming into the room, glared at Apple. "What

you doing up before lunch? You got to get your sleep, you'll be sick before this foolishness is over."

"I was half-asleep all last night," Apple told her. "Billy and I played pool till three in the morning at the Boat Club, all you could hear was our yawns. Listen, Frankie, will you cut out a dress for Cory so she can be in my wedding?"

"You've got your hands full already," Mrs. Mason said.

Frankie was considering Apple. She folded her hands on her apron and tipped her head forward, and Mrs. Mason saw the bobby pins which held her knotted hair to her head. "I believe I can do it," Frankie said slowly, "if I get started on it right now. Lunch is fixed, the table is set. Apple, you do the cleaning up. You all are going out for the rehearsal dinner —"

"Frankie, you'll be up all night." Mrs. Mason groaned.

Frankie told Apple, "You send Corinne down to the kitchen soon as she's finished her coffee so I can measure her." She went out.

Apple said to her parents, "I knew she'd do it."

"I think it's cruel of you to take advantage of her fondness for the girls." Mrs. Mason's voice trembled.

Mr. Mason said, "Darling, it'll be the thing she's proudest of when they ask for her accomplishments at the heavenly gate." He patted the small of his wife's back, then withdrew his hand as though she might lean on it. "I have to go see your Aunt Polly. You think maybe Corinne would come with me?"

"Not a chance," Apple said. "We need her here. And it wasn't cruel, it was kind," she told her mother crossly. "Frankie wants to be needed."

"More like taken advantage of!"

Apple looked at her mother. "Don't you want Corinne to be in my wedding?"

"No!" Mrs. Mason cried, and then she clamped her quivering lips.

"You know you don't mean that," Mr. Mason said.

"She's not well enough. She's never going to be well enough. Her bones feel as though they're going to bend."

"I'll put some starch in her," Apple said, and she strode out of the room.

Half an hour later, Frankie served the men working on the tent their second helpings and left the kitchen for the next door room, where she slept when Mrs. Mason needed her to spend the night. It was a concrete room with one window, covered with Virginia creeper that tinted the light.

Frankie took out her sewing box, pale blue plastic with many trays and compartments. She dove into the box and came up with a tape measure, which she flung over her shoulder. Then she stood waiting, looking at the door.

She heard Apple talking in the hall, and then Corinne came in, holding her white robe together at the neck. Apple said, behind her, "I'm leaving you here with Frankie, I have to make some calls."

Corinne lowered her chin and looked down at Frankie. For a minute the two women were silent. Then Frankie said, in a low voice, "Stand up straight and tuck your fanny under."

Corinne seemed to grow even taller as she eased the curve out of her spine. She dropped her hands to her sides and moved her feet a few inches farther apart. "Head back, like when you were a model," Frankie said, and Corinne tilted her chin. "Not that far!" Corinne lowered her chin till Frankie said, "There, keep that," and knelt on the floor at Corinne's bare feet.

"I was only a model that one time," Corinne said.

Frankie didn't answer. Reaching up, she passed the measuring tape around Corinne's waist.

"Oh, Frankie," Corinne said.

"Too tight?" Frankie asked, pulling. "We want that cummerbund to show off how little you are."

"It's not too tight," Corinne said.

"I don't need to measure your hips for that ballerina skirt," Frankie said. Quickly, she ran the tape from Corinne's waist to her ankle. "You're going to be wearing heels."

"I don't know."

"You're going to be wearing two-inch satin heels like Apple and the rest of them. We'll find you some."

"Apple said she'd find me some sandals."

"Tuck that tummy in," Frankie said. "Skinny as you are, you got a tummy," Then she passed the tape under Corinne's arms — "Lift up!" — and brought the two folds together on Corinne's chest. As the folds of the tape met, Frankie glanced at Corinne's eyes.

"Oh, Frankie," Corinne said, again.

"Don't start that foolishness," Frankie said. She dropped the tape, leaned down, and picked it up. "Now, hold out your arm. Wrist-length sleeves with that lace trim."

Finally she touched Corinne's shoulder, dismissing her. "You go up and rest till lunch."

13

As Corinne turned away, Frankie went to the bureau, opened a drawer, and rattled through layers of tissue paper. She pulled out a sheet of brown silk, the color of dead leaves. Shaking it out across her arm, she glanced at the doorway, where Corinne was slowly going into the hall, testing the floor with her toes like a timid swimmer at the edge of ice-cold water. Frankie frowned. Then her face smoothed, and she threw the silk across her cutting table.

Upstairs in the library, Apple was on the telephone. She sat hunched, one leg swinging, a cigarette clamped between two fingers. Now and then she tilted ashes into her empty coffee cup. "Frankie's making her dress right now," she said, and then, "Of course it'll be ready! You don't know Frankie."

A minute later, she said, "Don't be an idiot. Lila will understand, or she won't. I'm going to call her right now."

Then: "I don't know what you're talking about."

Finally, with exasperation: "What's a sad face at a wedding? She's my sister, Billy." She hung up the receiver with a sharp click and sat frowning at a silver patch of sun dancing on the wall. After a while she picked up the receiver again and dialed.

Meanwhile Mrs. Mason had gone to look at the tent. It was spread out on the grass; she leaned down and felt the grainy canvas. As she straightened up, she said aloud, "Where has the fun of it gone?" Dissatisfied with the word, she tried to think of another, but she hesitated to substitute *joy*. Yet it was joy she had felt, making her lists, starting her telephone calls, arranging each day to accomplish another step in the preparations for the wedding. She remembered the lesson she'd learned as a child: Jesus first, then others, finally yourself: joy.

"And now it's all ruined," she said, and saw Corinne's face floating up out of the grass, a pale daisy. Mrs. Mason turned sharply and went back to the house.

She stopped in the front hall and called, as though she was pitching her voice to the tops of trees, "Apple! Corinne! Lunchtime!" As in the old days, two doors opened and two sisters came out.

They followed her down the steps to the dining room, where Frankie had set out three green linen mats and three white plates with avocado-and-crabmeat salad. Mrs. Mason placed a daughter on either side and sat down at the head of the table.

"Now, nothing sad," she advised. "This is our last meal alone together."

Apple asked, "What's sad? I'm marrying an idiot tomorrow and it's too late to back out. I don't want to give back all the presents."

"Apple," her mother chided, cutting the avocado, which fell smoothly away from her silver knife. "Somebody might take you seriously."

"I am serious," Apple said, mashing her avocado.

Corinne, her hands in her lap, asked, "What did Billy do?"

"I'm not going to let you get away with not eating," Mrs. Mason warned her elder daughter.

"He said stupid things on the telephone. I had to hang up."

"What kind of stupid things?"

"Now, Apple, let your sister eat."

"He said he didn't want any sad faces at the wedding."

Corinne lifted her chin and looked at her sister.

"I told you he was a fool," Apple said. "I knew it when he said he understood why they shot those people at Kent State."

"Apple, you're going too far," Mrs. Mason said.

Corinne was still looking at her sister. "I don't think too much of Billy Long, but you know that."

"Yes, I know that," Apple said.

"I never would condone violence, but those students were in the wrong place," Mrs. Mason said.

"I wanted to see you marry somebody from away from here," Corinne told Apple.

"Like you?"

"I wanted to see you get out."

Mrs. Mason said, "Girls, it's not really the time —"

Apple interrupted her. "Don't worry, Cory. I'll get away from here. I'll come to live with you in New York City and we'll have an apartment full of women, parakeets, laundry, and other people's babies."

"That's not my view of your sister's life," Mrs. Mason said, a little desperately.

"No, it's her dream," Apple said. "Maybe my dream too, for all any of us knows."

There was a pause. "How is the dress coming along?" Mrs. Mason asked Corinne.

Apple said, "Frankie has started to cut."

After lunch, Apple rinsed the dishes and put them in the washer. Next door, Frankie's long shears slid through the silk. When Apple turned off the water, she heard the cutting and stood looking at her wet hands. The big diamond engagement ring winked at her through a haze of soapy water. She lifted her hands and shook them dry. Next door, the shears stopped, and Apple heard Frankie tear off a bit of silk.

Apple went upstairs to see if her mother and her sister were resting. Her mother's bedroom door was closed, which meant at least Mrs. Mason was lying down. Corinne's door was open a crack, and, looking in, Apple saw that her sister was not there. Then she heard the click of the dial on the telephone in the library.

"Hello?" Corinne said softly. "Operator? I want to call long distance."

A minute later, Apple heard her sister's voice rise and quaver: "Brian!"

She went into her room and slammed the door.

Mrs. Mason heard the slam and, confident that now both girls were resting, she looked at her bed. Frankie had made it that morning with the white embroidered blanket cover which Mrs. Mason always hesitated to turn back. There was something intimate about the appearance of a turned-down bed in the middle of the day. She glanced at the door. Then she slipped off her shoes and sat on the bed. After all, she was bound to have to answer the phone, unless Frankie got to it first. She leaned back stiffly against the pillows. Then, with a little sigh, she slid down and closed her eyes. Her hands were clenched at her sides, her toes pointed to the ceiling, and her eyelids wrinkled with the strain of staying closed.

Then someone knocked. Mrs. Mason's eyes flew open. "Who is it?" She sat up quickly.

"Can you talk?" Apple asked, coming in.

"Of course I can talk, darling. I was lying here thinking about the trip your father and I took to Italy the summer we were married."

"Your honeymoon?" Apple settled herself in the armchair near her mother's bed.

"That word has such connotations. We'd known each other since we were children, after all."

"Mother," Apple said, smiling, "what are you trying to tell me?"

"That I was a virgin on my wedding night, darling, and I wish to God you were going to be."

"Billy's not a virgin," Apple said. Mrs. Mason let that pass. "Anyway, that's not what I want to talk about. I want to ask you . . ." For the first time that day, Apple seemed to run out of breath. She looked at her mother, sitting on the edge of the bed. "Tell me how you made it work."

"What?"

"Marriage. Love."

Mrs. Mason carefully picked a hair off her daughter's shoulder. "I'll tell you one thing, I didn't start off offending my future sister-in-law."

"Cory comes first," Apple said.

"Well, it's too late to argue. You always do what you want."

"Tell me how you made it work," Apple repeated.

"Well. Remember when you were first going out in the evening? And I tried to tell you about sex? You were too young, you didn't understand. I tried to explain that sleeping together is what matters."

"I thought you were trying to stop me," Apple said.

"That, too. But that wasn't all. I was trying to teach you something. It's sleeping together that counts."

"Not love?" Apple asked. When her mother did not reply, Apple went on. "I think it only works if one person is sacrificed."

"We're talking about marriage, or I thought we were," her mother said dryly.

"Is that all?"

"All I can tell you that you'll accept. The other things — they're just words, to you. Loyalty. Fidelity. Absolute trust. Those are what I have with your father."

"And the greatest of these —" Apple murmured.

"Is fidelity."

Apple stood up. She went and looked out the window. "If he was always faithful to you, why do you resent Cory?"

"What!"

"I thought resentment came from jealousy," Apple said.

Mrs. Mason told her, "I have never resented, I never could resent your father's affection for his daughters."

"But what about the way he loves Cory?"

Mrs. Mason also stood up. "Young lady, you are getting in way over your head."

Apple whipped around. The two women were close. "Don't you know why she's ruined?"

"Nobody's ruined in this house," Mrs. Mason said.

"She's ruined by men, for men," Apple said. "You know that. You feel it in her. Some rottenness. Some soft place, where they always bore. You said her bones would bend. I say it's a bruised spot, a rotten spot that came when you first started to hate her."

"I don't want you to talk this way to me," Mrs. Mason said. "You are upset about the wedding, all brides are. Go away and get ahold of yourself." She pushed one foot into a shoe. "I have to see about the tent."

"Don't you care that she's ruined?" Apple asked.

Mrs. Mason slipped on the other shoe. "I still believe things will work out for Corinne. And now if you will let me pass —"

Apple stood aside. Mrs. Mason went rapidly into the hall and opened the front door. As she closed it behind her, she gasped, once, then shut her lips and hurried towards the tent.

It was rising, inching shakily up its guidelines. She heard Harvey roar as one section, probably Pete's, dipped towards the ground. There was a faltering, and then the tent started to rise again, white as sails, yellow as sun against the magnolias.

Mrs. Mason clapped her hands. "It's worth it. It's all worth it," she said aloud. And for the rest of the afternoon, her face was satisfied as she went about her last-minute chores, checking the shined silver, counting the cake plates, arranging flowers in the other guest room. Only at the end of the day, before supper, when she went out to pick poppies for the altar and saw her husband bend to singe their stems with his lighter, to keep the sap in, and noticed, perhaps for the first time, the way he trembled, straightening up — only then, with the red cups of the poppies blazing between

them, did she allow herself to wonder. Silly! she thought.
And her lips trembled.

"I suppose Billy will get over the change," she remarked
to Mr. Mason.

"It'll be the first of many, living with Apple!"

Their eyes met, over the poppies, and a shadow passed
between them, a pledge of silence. Behind them, in the
house, Frankie turned on the sewing machine light.

$\mathscr{A}$PPLE'S AUNT POLLY asked on her official visit, "William Long, where in the world did you two meet?" Right then, I couldn't remember where I first saw Apple — Adeline, to give her her real name, which she will use when we are married. Here names turn into nicknames and back again like rabbits jumping in and out of hats, but no one is confused. Apple's kind knows everyone in this town, has always known everyone, from the kids in the swimming pool, arms and legs thrashing, some parent holding them up, to the faces coming out of the crowd on the dance floor. Still, sometimes even they have to ask, "Who in the world is that?" to sort a face out of the general brew.

Her family kept Apple apart: "closely held," I call it. They didn't believe in private clubs and schools, and so Apple got her early education at the public school on Bluff Road with the children of the people who sell fishing worms. After a few years of that, her mother sent her to Trinity School for Girls, but by then she was already different. For one thing, she didn't have anywhere to swim or take tennis lessons, so she had to invent things to do on her own: riding her bike "to hell and gone," she told me, meaning across the county line, making pictures with magnolia petals on a garden bench — that kind of thing. She might have turned out silent and shy if it hadn't been for her family's traveling habit: every summer, she had to train for a trip to Europe, which meant more long dresses than a country club summer and learning to make conversation when the purser broke in.

Still trying to remember the first time I noticed her, I remembered that summer when I was riding the little circuit — county horse shows, that kind of thing. I had a black gelding saddle horse I thought was pretty special, although he didn't measure up in the ring — he was feisty, bad-acting, didn't respond well to commands. I was determined to win me some ribbons to justify the money I'd spent at the old Rock Creek Stables, learning how to ride. I had sense enough to stick to the small-time — white fences around dry rings, the lights at night swarming with moths, a few spectators, drinking beer. One of those nights, her family for some reason took her — oh yes, they'd been to visit the negro church on Rose Island Road; her father's a liberal the way they can only be here, big as end-of-summer zucchini, uneatable but striking. For a treat, they dropped by after the church to see the fair.

I'd done badly in the show and was foul-tempered coming out of the ring with Sat — that was his name, short for Saturn, don't you know. He was lathered white! Here they were by the gate, a posy of a family, each one in place. I stopped to speak, and her father introduced us. I think I had seen her one time before, in church, but then she was still wearing white socks.

Not quite grown-up but pretty in that melting ice-cream way you know may not outlast the first baby. (I'll have to see to that: exercise classes, regular beauty-parlor appointments.) Little blond threads of hair, a pink face, blue eyes like her father's and nipples I could see through her blouse. Brown legs — legs that could ride and swim and run, not the spikes of party girls. The rump I wasn't sure of. Those days girls wore full skirts and cinch belts. On horseflesh and womenflesh, the tail end means a lot to me. I decided to find out.

I went off with Sat, pretty sure that those high, hot lights on my hair and his foamy hide did something — a little — for me. Apple kept a diary with a gold key (I learned that later) and of that night would write, "As we passed the ring, a man and a horse in a cooling sheet came up to us; the man tipped his hat. In the half light, I saw only the dark and white of his riding habit yet the very austerity of colors attracted me; I felt as though he had made a statement composed of two simple, enormously important words."

Well! I waited a couple of days, to let Apple start to wonder, and then I telephoned. The old negro cook they'd had "all their lives" — that's the way they talk; it's the length of the service that makes it OK — answered the telephone and then went off for a long time. I imagined the receiver swinging at the end of its cord, slow circles in the kitchen, where the lights would have been turned off to keep it cool.

After about five minutes, Apple came to the telephone and explained that she'd been out on the tin roof, sunbathing, and Frankie had had to holler all over the house. After that, there wasn't anything I could say that wouldn't be anticlimactic, so I just asked her to go to the movies on Friday. I'd planned something short and simple that wouldn't get her hopes up. I was pretty sure Apple would throw two or three monkey wrenches into any plan of mine if I gave her half a chance. I already knew I wanted to marry her.

You will ask, How? So quick? Just the way Mother and Lila did later when I told them. I guess the best I can do by way of explanation is to say that there comes a time and a place and the girl sort of drops into them. I know that doesn't sound too flattering to Apple, but I don't mean it that way. I was two years out of business school and doing all right at River City Hardware, her father's plant; I had my gelding, the first of many, my weekend life following the horse shows. I'd run through quite a few girls in my time, run through them pretty literally — Mother used to accuse me of that when they started calling at all hours of the night — but I didn't care about that kind of thing anymore. I mean, it had gotten to the point where I could tell when — and I mean exactly when — a new girl was going to let me put my tongue in her mouth (usually at the end of the first date) and when she was going to let me get my hands inside her blouse (usually at the end of the second date). Where is the fun in that?

Fun's the wrong word, anyway. I wasn't looking for fun but for some first-rate solid material. Apple had that. Was that. All she needed — was crying out for — was somebody to take her in hand.

You've seen that if you know anything about horses: a

well-bred filly, a year old, half-broke, soured by stupid handling, running wild in a field. You call to her, whistle, and
she comes up, blowing, skids in a dirt spray ten feet off and
looks at you sideways. You hold out a handful of oats and
she passes two or three times, trotting so delicate, eyeing
you. Finally she swerves around and darts her long head
out, lifts her lip, and swipes the oats — not ladylike, not
gentle, but thieving and jumping away with a wild red in
her eye. That filly has breeding. Her legs are sound. Her
disposition — you wouldn't give anything for her disposition, right then, because she's been neglected and spoiled
rotten at the same time.

But the good material's there, you can feel it in her, and
you know you have to start by learning her to bear your
hand on her neck. It'll be a slow process, she'll take firm
handling (coaxing, too, but that's easy; it's the firm handling
that's tricky, you have to steel your heart), but in the end —
even if it takes years — you'll have a mount that's first-class
because you started with breeding — quality — and nothing but a lifetime of bad treatment, if that, can damage pure
quality. Bloodlines, they call it in the horse business, but
with people, it's pretty much the same; you look at the dam
and the sire and you see the class, the strength, the blood
itself showing in the way they look you straight in the eye,
hold out their hands, invite you in.

Well, considering all that, I got a shock on our first date.
I expected complaints about the movie, grousing about this
boring little town where we couldn't find a place open for
a drink at 10:00 P.M. I got that, and double. Apple had just
come back from one of those jaunts with her family, had

spent months combing Ireland, doing everything but riding; she said there'd been no time but I guessed she was afraid. She said she hated to come back to this podunk town that smelled like the inside of a vacuum cleaner bag. She'd had one year of Jefferson Junior College, which was beneath her, and was itching to get loose. They didn't send her East to college because in those days East-to-college was reserved for those we all knew were going there anyway. She was still festering over that slight and spent a long time telling me she had every intention of going to graduate school in New York or Boston, getting some kind of degree — she wasn't sure which kind — that would give her a start in "publishing." I didn't know what she meant by that but figured it was magazines.

I told her a little about Sat, how we'd spent the weekends going from show to show, not winning but enjoying the competition. (I didn't tell her how much I'd wanted to win.) She half-listened. I didn't expect more; girls with Apple's looks don't have to do more than half-listen. And I swear the tan skin on her arm flinched when I touched her the way Sat's flinches when he's trying to dislodge a fly.

That didn't discourage me. I kind of liked her for being so hard to entertain.

Then I took her home. It was a full-moon night; the big maples around her house were alive with fireflies. We got out of the car at the same time — she wasn't one to sit and wait while I went to open her door — and then, without saying a word, we both started down the hill. Her mother's garden was off to the left, and we wandered in there, feeling our way in the thick dark. I said, "You've got to be very quiet so you won't disturb the night noises," and then I put my arms around her and kissed her, to shut her up. She sighed and laid her head on my shoulder like a tired child. I would have rocked her, that would have been fine, but all of a sudden, she started up and wanted to kiss me again — this time, hard, with her teeth more than her lips. My head went back. Then she reached for my fly.

I took her hand off. She was beginning some expert manipulation of my zipper. "I don't want you to do that," I said. I'd never get anywhere if I let her take charge.

"What's the matter? Don't you like me?"

"Where did you pick up that line?"

"I thought you were attracted to me."

"I'm attracted to you, Apple. You're a pretty girl."

"I'm not a girl, I'm a woman," she said.

"That remains to be seen, but I'm not going to have any rolling around on the wet grass, then home and forget about it."

"You think I'm promiscuous," she said, savoring the word.

"I wouldn't know."

"I am promiscuous," she said, giving it all its juice. "I like to go to bed with boys. Men."

"You're free to choose, but I don't like to go to bed with girls."

She turned away and darted towards the house, and I had to run to catch her. I ran with my heart pounding, my breath burning my throat — I was in shape, but she was fast as a whippet. She couldn't get her key in the lock quick enough, though; I caught her by the back of the neck.

28

"Let go," she said, twisting.

I held on. "I don't want you to hang up on me when I call. I'll take you riding."

"I've been riding all my life."

"Ever done any jumping?"

"No."

"It might scare you. We could start with cavallettis . . ."

"I've been going over cavallettis since I was ten years old," she said, and I let her go. She turned her key in the lock, went inside, and closed the door in my face. But I knew when I called she wouldn't hang up. And that was important to me. Too important. I didn't want her to know. A girl like Apple gets bored with things that come too easily.

She didn't hang up, but she had evidently decided to force me to do what she wanted to do, on our next date, so when I suggested the drive-in, she tittered (I hope I never have to use that word for her laugh again, but in this case, it was appropriate) and said she'd prefer to go riding. I knew they had some kind of backyard horses, had ridden since they were kids in the sloppy way people do here, just to get out and around, not caring how it's done or whether the horses are well-treated or barely maintained. It wasn't the kind of riding that interested me, but I was curious to see how she'd perform, and curious for another reason, too: I hadn't seen her yet in pants. So I told her I'd drop by after work the next day.

That afternoon I left River City Hardware the same time as her father, and I told him, on the way to the parking lot, that I was going to see his daughter. Mr. Mason looked hotter and more wrinkled than I was used to seeing him; he bent to unlock his car and said, "You know, Billy, in twenty years I've never once locked my car. Last week somebody took my camera — just a little old Brownie box — out of the backseat, and of course since then I've been locking up. I'm going to reach mandatory retirement in five years — you know I always follow my own rules — and I'll be locking my car every single day of the week until then."

I said, "That's too bad, sir."

"This town is changing. Did you hear Levy's Department Store is being sold to an out-of-towner? Somebody from Cincinnati? Eli Levy started that store the same year — 1887 — my great-grandfather started River City. They built the two buildings to be in harmony — Wallace Steele designed them both." Levy's is red brick and gothic trim and River City is a square of white limestone, but I could see what he meant: each building takes up an entire city block, and they face each other like the two walls of a mountain pass.

"So you're going to see my daughter," he added, as an afterthought. "I didn't know you two knew each other."

"You introduced me to Adeline at the horse show," I reminded him.

"Apple, we call her. What are you two going to do?"

"Go riding, she says."

"Apple's had that pony since she was twelve years old. I don't know how she can still ride him; her legs must hang down to the ground. Will we be seeing you for supper?"

"I don't want to impose —"

"Mrs. Mason will be crushed if you drive all the way out

there and then go home with nothing to eat. I believe she's planning chicken and broccoli."

"I'd be delighted."

He hopped into his car, closed the door, and rolled the window down. "Is that a promise, now?"

I promised, then wondered if he was really all that eager to marry Apple off. It would take some explaining if he was. She was barely nineteen, and there was no reason to think she would hang long on the vine.

Driving out of town, it struck me maybe Mr. Mason was lonely.

He lived in a house of women, the way I did, with Mother and Lila, and I knew from my own experience how wearing that can be. Even their attentions get you down, after a while. Hardly a day passes that Mother doesn't ask me what I want for supper, though I'm hardly in the mood at eight o'clock in the morning to start thinking about supper. Then she'll pout because I haven't expressed "adequate interest."

My sister Lila has the same problem. She's an RN at Baptist Hospital, and she doesn't have much time to bother with family routine. "Just throw me a fried egg," she'll say when Mother starts about her menus. "I have to be Out There at seven o'clock this evening." She calls the hospital Out There: Mother calls it Out There, too, although it's actually closer to town than we are. But it's a mixed bag, that hospital; they take all kinds, not necessarily Baptists, and some of the Baptists are strange enough.

So as I was saying, it's possible Mr. Mason wanted me so hard because otherwise he'd only have hens at his table.

While I was leafing through all these thoughts, I'd taken

31

Bluff Road and was driving past the sand company, with its peaked mountains of coarse gray river sand — the kind they used to put in park sandboxes when I was a kid. The river got into everything, in the old days. Those sandboxes were one of its signs. In the hot summers, we didn't have any-where to swim — like Apple, though for different reasons, we didn't belong to clubs — and so I used to go down to the river, at the foot of Fourth Street, about every afternoon between May and October. Mother had a horror of the locks; she said grown men had been swept into them and ground up against the walls. I never told her I swam fifty feet up-stream from McCintock — the largest — because the water was clearer there; I think there must have been an under-ground spring. Also I liked to see the big E. T. Slider tugs come barreling down the river, tooting for the lockkeeper, who'd time it so the lock doors would open, smooth as butter, just as the first barge came flying through.

Nobody swims or fishes in the river anymore. There are chemical wastes coming down from Cincinnati that would rip the skin off your bones. You can't inoculate against them the way you could against typhoid. The only things alive in the river now are enormous eels, ten or twelve feet long, and even the negroes won't fool with them. The river has gotten to be like an alley running in back of a row of houses, useful as a place where garbage can be thrown but with no more influence on people than the stink that comes up on a hot day when people say, "That river!" as though they'd forgotten about it since the last spell of hot weather.

I was driving past Fox Park, which has been taken over by the negroes. There was a softball team practicing with a

big black buck crouching behind the plate and a whole
swarm of women and children watching. They had brought
practically everything they owned — mongrels and baby
carriages and tables and chairs. They were going to spend
the evening like they were at home, shouting and carrying
on over the game, drinking beer and lemonade, starting up
fires, barbecuing, talking, eating, singing — maybe even
cleaning up. I don't have anything against negroes; I was
raised with them, went to school in a two-thirds black neighborhood because we couldn't afford to live anywhere else
till my father died and the life insurance bought us our
gatehouse. I guess I could even say that some of my best
friends . . . Well, I guess not quite. But I do have respect
for them. They make their lives up out of darn little. You
have to have had nothing yourself to know the effort that
takes. Still, I get hot under the collar when I see the way
they've made themselves at home in Fox Park. I mean, when
it was dedicated, it was meant to be for everybody. Mr.
Mason made the speech.

He'd been "instrumental" — how I love that word! — in
having the park laid out on top of the city dump, and he'd
donated a big pair of brick gates from some old place for
the entrance. The sign over the top is two hands, shaking —
that's our state symbol . . . and the name, Fox Park, in big
letters on a background of curled iron leaves.

Soon I was driving through long, flat fields that flood
regularly from January to March and show the results: the
best corn for miles around. The rainy summer had grown
the corn so high some of the stalks were toppling, and I'd
heard talk of wilt. I slowed down to get a look at the ears,

and they were filling out nicely. I've promised myself that when I get my own land, I'll put in a couple of acres of corn. There's nothing like the shine and rustle of those leaves.

One of the really high-class subdivision roads led off next. It's called Lakota Hills, and by that logic I was beginning to understand, they don't even have a sign. It looks like a little old country road. I'd been back there for deb parties — it's wonderful, I always tell Mother, what you can do with a rented tux — and I knew those houses are mostly 'twenties and 'thirties Georgians and Tudors with two-acre lawns, big garages, and maybe a child's playhouse or a vegetable garden out back. Comfortable — that's one of Mother's favorite words — and that word fits Lakota Hills. I wouldn't want to live there, though. There isn't enough to mark one house off from the next.

Apple — I started to think about her then — would do just about anything to make a place stand out. That was not what I wanted of her, and in fact it seemed to me I'd have to keep a pretty close watch on her to be sure she didn't take it upon herself to stand out, anyway.

Finally I got to the big curve in the river where the old lighthouse stands. It's a red light on a rickety wooden structure that looks like a big stepladder. I never have known who tends the light, turns it off and on; it's one of the few ways we still recognize the river, although it carries more barge traffic than the Mississippi. I always slow down and give that light a nod.

Then I came to Apple's gates, and they still make me smile. Those people live behind two plain old white wooden posts that look like they might lead to a truck farm with a crusty tenant house. Why Mr. Mason with his "position in the community" — that's another phrase I'm fond of — chooses to live behind those two posts is beyond me. Mother would be able to explain it; she has a lot of faith in what she calls the old way. To me, it seems ridiculous.

I bumped along over the dirt road with Queen Anne's lace and ironweed brushing my elbow. It looked to me as though those front fields hadn't been cut in a long time. They were growing up with volunteer pines, flowering Judas, crab apple, and honeysuckle that would take it all in another few years. I wondered if they thought it looked picturesque; it looked wasteful, to me.

The frame house was not large or pretentious. A good setting for my Apple, I thought as I parked. You'll notice I was already saying "my" — shameless, Mother would call it. One of the things I like about myself is that I'm pretty direct.

The big box bushes by the front door were leaning in as though in a few more years they'd meet and block access; the magnolias on the other side of the walk had escaped winter kill: big needle-shaped soft seedpods and not a brown leaf to be seen. I walked up to the door and looked for a knocker or a bell. There was no knocker or bell. I opened the door and walked in.

Inside, I stopped dead. There was Mrs. Mason, a few feet from me, with her back turned, fixing flowers. She's a small woman, about Apple's size — five feet three and a half, I'd say, and weighing maybe a hundred and fifteen pounds, five more than her younger daughter. Little fish bones in her ankles and her elbows, little feet in black-strapped

35

high-heeled shoes — dressed to do the flowers the way most women dress for a party.

She was arranging some tall, spike-shaped blue flowers — delphiniums, I think they were — and singing to herself, the old song about False Sir John a-wooing came. I would have preferred another. I cleared my throat, and she looked around.

"I hated to just march in, but I didn't see a bell," I told her.

"We never have had one." She stared at me, a delphinium spike in one hand, and I realized — it's a familiar feeling — that as well as I knew who she was, I was a total stranger to her. I introduced myself, and even then there was a bad wait before she edged up a smile and said, "You must be looking for Apple."

"Yes," I said. "She's going to show me her horse."

"Pony," Mrs. Mason corrected me, turning back to put some black-spotted orange lilies in with the delphiniums. "Apple has had that beast since she was twelve years old; I think it's a he, or altered — I'm never sure about those things!" She looked at me as though I was going to set her straight. "A fine life Apple has led him," she added, to make me see the comparison.

"I can't believe Apple would be inconsiderate to animals," I said, to give her a laugh.

She took it: a little gurgle, like a water fountain. "I'm not sure I would trust Apple to that extent! But you young men are all alike. You think a pretty face stands for a sweet disposition. It's more complicated than that, I can assure you. And then," she added, "Apple has so many interests." She looked at me to see if I was one of them.

36

"I'm barely a friend, right now," I told her. "I hope to be more than a friend, one day, if your daughter will let me."

She stared at me, standing there like an announcing angel with that devil-colored lily in her hand. "You mean you want to be taken seriously?"

"I do," I said.

Suddenly she knew who I was. "You're Cora Long's boy, aren't you? She used to raise the prettiest petunias. We talked about them at church: how these new hybrids are too ruffled. She still fooling with flowers?"

"She's lost interest in them, the last few years, with my sister and me both still living at home. She concentrates on vegetables now. You can feed three people off one big summer squash."

"No protein," Mrs. Mason said and turned away to make it clear she was through talking.

"How do I get to the barn?" I asked her.

"Go down the hill and turn left at the triangle." She didn't even look at me when I left.

I walked down the road to what they called the triangle, a piece of wild growth, and took the left turn to the barn. It was a tin-roofed wreck like something a tenant farmer had let fall down over the years, windowsills slanting and the few glass panes that were left riddled with BB shots. One big sliding door hung off its top hinge. Inside I smelled a century of manure.

"Apple!" I called.

"Come back here," she yelled from the far end.

She was slapping a saddle on an old gray pony.

"Hello," I said, knowing better than to kiss her.

"Hello," she said in her gruff way, as though she was a

middle-aged woman, living with a female friend, finished with men for the last generation.

She was wearing a boy's pink oxford shirt with the cuffs rolled up and the front buttoned to her chin. "Don't just stand there!" she told me. "Get the bridle."

I went into what she without a doubt called the tack room and found a stiffened old double-rein hackamore hanging on a nail. I brought it to her. "You don't take much trouble with your tack, do you? This needs a good saddle soaping."

"I only do the tack when it rains and it's been dry since May," she said, snatching the bridle out of my hand. She rammed those two bits between the pony's peeled lips and slapped him when he backed, rolling his eyes. When she went to tighten the girth, that pony bloated. She drew back her foot to give him a kick, and I said, "Apple."

"How'd you find your way over here?" she asked, putting her foot down.

"I've been here a few times, to parties."

She jerked the girth tighter, pulled the stirrup down, pushed her toe in, and hopped up — it wasn't far. She adjusted her leathers and got her feet into position, standing up to test them; she had a pretty seat. Even on that dwarf pony, she didn't look ridiculous.

He pulled away and pattered out of the barn, tried to balk at the gate to the ring but she jabbed him through. "Shut the gate!"

I did, and leaned on it to watch her. She was sitting OK, maybe a little too far forward, but that was better than the other way around. She had that lazy pony trotting fast on a loose rein. Her hands were light, but she was holding them high. "Drop your hands," I called.

She dropped them right down on the saddle.

"You know that's not what I mean."

She left them there and kicked the pony into a choppy canter. She was bouncing stiffly, and I called, "Sit back! You're almost on his neck."

She rewarded me as I might have expected, by laying out flat on the pony's crupper.

I had to laugh, watching her. She had a flexible spine.

Next time around, I climbed the gate and reached out and grabbed that pony's rein. He reared back, glaring. Apple's expression as she sat up more or less matched.

"You don't want me to tell you anything, do you?" I asked her.

"Look, I ride the way I want. If it's not right, I don't give a shit."

"Have it your own way," I said. "I thought you wanted me to teach you how to jump."

"I told you, I know how to jump," she said, and I said — there was no way around it, "All right. Show me."

She ran that pony around to the other side of the ring, turned him, and, digging her heels in, started back. I had no idea what she had in mind, and it wasn't until that beast was almost on top of me that I stepped out of the way. She yelled and jabbed him at the last minute, and the pony gathered his short legs up — I wouldn't have believed it was possible — and heaved himself over the gate, a good four feet. I saw Apple fly past, flat out on his neck, and then I heard that pony thump down on the other side. Apple was hanging on to his mane, jolted out of the saddle, one stirrup swinging. Little Mischief started lickety-split for the barn.

She'd lost a rein, and I saw that devil was going to clip

39

her knee on the side of the door. I ran after her, caught the rein, and pulled him in. She was red in the face but not ready to thank me. "What'd you do that for?"

"To save your kneecap. That was quite a jump. They'd never give you any ribbons for horsemanship."

"I didn't do it for horsemanship."

"Look, if you'd let me give you a few pointers . . ."

She slid down. We were about three inches apart. I could smell the hot hairs on the back of her neck, imagined I could smell the blond wax in her ear. I wanted to put my tongue inside the first curve where the cartilage, turning over, looks transparent, like a shell.

"All right," she said. "You can give me some pointers, next time. As long as you know I know how to do it already." She did smile.

She took the saddle off and brushed past me, rammed that saddle over a barrel in the tack room, came back and took me by the shoulders, and kissed me, as though it was some kind of responsibility.

I stood back and wiped my mouth on my hand. "You kiss like a can opener," I said.

"That's the way I like to." She went back to the pony and slipped off his bridle, giving him the first pat I'd seen. The beast peeled back his lips and would have bitten her, through that pink sleeve to the bone, if she hadn't snatched her arm out of the way. She cursed him and slapped him, and he took off, dodging into the pasture. She ran after him to slam the gate.

When she came back, she said to me, "I like to start things. You'll have to get used to that."

40

It was the second sentence I preferred. She seemed to be referring to a future.

Still, I was annoyed. I followed her out of the barn, swearing I'd take ahold of the situation.

I nearly, very nearly told her right then about Corinne.

We were passing a bunch of shabby-looking pines beside her mother's garden, Apple still keeping the lead on me, striding as fast as she could go. I hated the feeling of trying to catch up with her, and it was on the edge of my lips to say, "You see those pines? That's where your sister Corinne and I —" That would have ruined everything.

I managed to get ahold of my temper, and then I took her arm. "Your father invited me to stay for supper, but I don't want to do it if it'll aggravate you," I said.

"I'd be delighted," Apple said, slowing down, and I felt her toothpick arm give way inside my grip. That did it. I'd wanted proof that she'd respond — finally, finally — to my grip on her, and she'd given it to me. It was all I could ask for on a second date.

CHAPTER THREE

RS. MASON asked me around four, "Have you started the chicken?" knowing of course I had because that was what was written down for Thursday. We have that talk every afternoon. "Are you doing the broccoli? Have you started the new potatoes?" I think she gets the taste of them in her mouth, when we go over them that way.

She was sitting on her chair, the long one, with her feet up and the baby shawl over them. I'd asked when the two girls were grown, "What do we do with these things?" meaning the yellow-and-white boxes with all those little clothes. She picked through them, one day, going and coming — I heard her feet on the floor, over my head in the kitchen — and finally laid out five little dresses, the hand-made ones. And the blue baby blanket, "For my feet" — I didn't know then what she meant. Then she asked me if I could use the rest of the clothes. I said I didn't know anybody good enough for all those lace-edged bibs and fancy pink and white sunsuits — those were the days! I don't need a picture to remember the girls dressed up, pretty babies, both, but Apple the one I always wanted to take and keep by me for a bad time.

Mrs. Mason wants me always to say yes — but I learned the hard way to say yes only when I could stick to it. First years with her, I said yes to make her smile, then ended up half the time trying to take it back. I learned fast in those days, learned she didn't just want to hear the sound of the word, the way I thought; she wanted to see that yes dance, overhead, in sunbeams.

I don't know what she did with all those little dresses. Called the Goodwill, I guess, on my day off — "not to embarrass Frankie." I've heard that a lot. Goodwill probably turned them into rags, or else there's a lot of fancy-dressed cracker babies in those rooming houses on Seventh Street.

Coming back to her, today, and the dinner, I repeated what she told me to make for dessert . . . floating island — and she nodded, satisfied, as though I'd given her a spoonful. She eats so little at regular mealtimes she has to eat between; bird-boned body, the same it was when he first brought her here. I thought then, she'll break, but she never has, or bent, either.

I went down to stuff the chicken — we like to use our own bread crumbs, made from stale bread; we like to use our own herbs, out of her garden, picked every fall and hung up in the basement to dry. So that takes a little time: stuffing. Nobody eats it, but she says she hates the naked way a roasting hen looks with that gaping hole.

Parsley, too. I went out to the garden to cut a bunch, heard her upstairs, moving around — the windows were open — and wondered if she would come out, now the heat was off the trees.

I stopped to look at that river. Never have been a big fan of the Ohio, but that evening it was silver as the side of a fish, laid out flat, and the big tulip poplars in the valley were holding shade, shine, and leaves. The view is getting grown up, there's only a patch of it left, compared to twenty years ago, but she doesn't want to cut those trees. They've grown up with us, she says, they've taken the sap of our lives in their roots — she'll say that kind of thing, sometimes, when she's calling-herself-helping in the kitchen.

I took that parsley back in. She'd come down and was tying on that pink apron.

"You ought to go out, see that river," I said. "It's silver."

"July evenings. I like them the best. August is too hot, of course, and I can't stand that dry smell in the fall." She tied the apron string with a big loop, so she could get her finger in and pull it undone fast. "Let me chop that parsley."

My kitchen cabinets are full of little machines and plastic gadgets — I don't fool with them. She took one of them out and put the parsley in it — it was a jar with an orange top and a handle — and cranked that handle and out the parsley came, minced fine. "I could do that with a knife," I said.

"No, you couldn't. Not and have it come out this way."

"Well, give it to me, I want to get this bird stuffed and in the oven."

She watched me mix in the parsley. "You using the salt substitute?"

"When I don't forget."

"It's Mr. Mason's health, Frankie."

"That salt substitute doesn't do a thing for the food."

"No," she said, "but what difference does that make? I mean, in the balance. If he goes ahead of me, I won't go on; you remember that, Frankie, when the time comes."

"Go along. You too young." It's about the only time I drop into that talk. "Young, and just as pretty!" It sounded rusty.

"Not with two grown daughters. They'll be making me a grandmother soon!"

"Miss Apple not studying children. Miss Corinne —"

"She'll make a wonderful mother." She took an onion and ran it through her little jar.

"I don't need no more onion." I opened the oven and put in the bird.

"I'll wrap it up, you can use it tomorrow." She slid the plastic wrap out of the drawer. "You going to set the table?"

"You want the pink mats?" We use them every weeknight: pale pink shell-shaped mats, with little tears she's darned with white thread.

"Yes, and the candelabra."

"It's not shined."

"I'll shine it," she said, and went under the sink for the rubber gloves. I loaded the tray with linen, china, and glasses while she wrenched the top off the gray dauby silver polish — one job I hate. She does just about all of it, though you wouldn't know it, to hear her speak about that closetful of silver — "as tarnished as an old dime."

I went in the dining room to lay the table. There the river was, outside the windows. I stopped and looked at it again and wondered why when I see it six days a week — or call

45

myself seeing it; mostly I don't notice — it was only tonight the silver shine would strike me so I couldn't set my table. It was that flat look. The Ohio's a treacherous river — I know scads who've drowned there — and usually it lets you see that: that gray greasy color doesn't just come from mud. Now, it had a peaceful look, a summer look that could have fooled even me.

I went back in the kitchen. "You want salad plates?"

She said, "Frankie, you know we use salad plates every time we have a salad. How many years —"

"Twenty-five, come January nineteenth."

"Why, we weren't even unpacked yet; you served us our first dinner sitting on packing cases and we had salad plates. Those green Ming dynasty copies that got chewed up in the washing machine —"

"The summer I was sick and you hired that Rosie —"

"Didn't have enough sense not to put Ming dynasty copies in the washing machine. I like these cabbage-leaf better." She was handing them down, off the cabinet shelf.

"I was looking at the river," I said. "It's changed its stripes."

"You looking at the river and me shining silver."

"Changed its stripes like it's quit drowning people."

"It never will quit drowning people, Frankie."

"I got to start my water for the broccoli," I told her. "Another pot for the potatoes." I looked at my stove while I was turning on the burners; it gives me satisfaction. Big and black and built the way stoves used to be — gas even though the electric man told her there wouldn't be any gas left for stoves in another year. The all-electric kitchen: they sell them in one piece. Everything matching in some bright color. "I like my old gas stove, you can keep an even flame under a pot," she said, looking at me, speaking my words as though she did the cooking as well as the talking; and she can only heat soup, my day off.

She won't let them in to paint the kitchen, either, won't even let me sew up rickrack curtains, red, green, or white: says a kitchen ought to look like what it is, a workroom. So we have the old black-and-white checked linoleum we started out with, the rubber mat by the sink, the big deal table with the tin top, the marble for my pastry, the warming oven standing high on its steel legs, the old rattan chairs, and the glass-fronted cabinets where you can see all her precious possessions. That's the only kind of kitchen I'll ever cook in — I've told her that.

"You'll leave us one fine day," she said after Cory's wedding, "and nobody will know why or where."

"You'll have a long wait if you plan on waiting for that."

We were putting away the wedding dress: layers of tissue paper, a special box that smelled like paste.

"Someday, Frankie, the new times are going to catch up with you and me. Hand me that string."

"With you, maybe. Not with me."

Now I didn't say that to make her smile but because it's the God's own truth. When Wilson's sister — she's supposed to be my best friend — starts out at me about how lucky I am, with my "family," I always hush her up. They're not my family and never will be, not even Apple, who I raised from a baby seven days old. I don't hold with that kind of nonsense. They are the people I work for. They pay me well, and regular — have never missed a Sunday, or asked me to stay late without warning. They are the people I work for. Isn't that enough? What more can you expect, in this life?

Miss Apple came in then. I call her Miss when she has that look: walking fast, swinging her arms like she was rowing herself through thick air. She was in one big hurry — flashed by the kitchen table, turned half around, and pecked a kiss at her mother. "What is it now?" Mrs. Mason asked, staring; you could always tell, with Apple, when something was up. Even when she was a little bit of a girl, she never twisted her dress or stood her foot on one side; she looked you in the eye and *asked*.

"Can Billy Long stay to supper?"

Mrs. Mason looked scared. "All we've got is roasting chicken. I'm afraid he'll starve."

"He doesn't care about eating. He wants to be with us. You haven't even met him."

"I've met Billy Long. He came to one of Corinne's big parties, the year she made her debut."

"How come you didn't tell me before?" Apple pulled a slice of cucumber from under my knife and ate it, skin and all.

"You'll get a bellyache. That skin is full of wax," I told her. She took another slice.

"You like him?" she asked her mother.

Mrs. Mason was too smart to be run into that corner. "Who? Billy Long? Why, I hardly know him!"

"Thought you said you met him at —"

"A deb party? Five hundred people, under a striped tent? I wouldn't call that knowing!"

48

Apple gave a big sigh. "Look, can he stay to supper?"

"Of course he can stay, darling." She put her hand on Apple's shoulder and kissed her. "You going to change out of those sweaty clothes?"

"He can't change," Apple said.

"Yes, but, honey, you've been on horseback, and it's hot."

Apple, for once, took her mother's way. "All he did was watch — you're right. Never sweated a drop. I'll go take a shower in Daddy's bathroom. He's not home yet, is he?"

"Run along, darling, you've got plenty of time." Mrs. Mason said to me, a minute later, "I always meant to have a shower put in the girls' bathroom, but now with Corinne gone and Apple —"

"They like they daddy's bath," I said, dropping into that talk again.

"Yes, but they leave it a mess, the mirror so steamed up he can't see to shave, wet towels balled up all over the floor, puddles because they never will put the shower curtain inside."

"Miss Apple ain't that bad."

She laughed. "I have a kind of an idea, Frankie, she won't be with us that much longer."

"She's got the rest of the summer to get through, and then she's going back to the — what do you call it?"

"Community college. It's not much. She says it's mainly nurses."

"Miss Apple never cared a thing about books," I said, dipping the tomatoes in my potato water (which was boiling) and shucking off the skins. "Now if you want to talk about Miss Corinne —"

"I don't know what good books ever did her."

"Three of them — big and fat! — in her suitcase when she came home for her wedding."

"Crying so much she wouldn't have been able to see to read."

"Miss Corinne going to be all right." I gave it as much force as I could muster. "Settle down, have her a baby —"

"Yes, she's going to be all right," she said, looking at me and nodding. "You mark my words! They all have to go through their difficult times: you remember when we were trying to train Apple —"

"Would go on the floor on the way to the pot — hold her little skirt up, and laugh!"

"And Corinne, now, in New York — that's not her kind of place. She doesn't have a relative there. Well, she'll have to make herself a life. It is taking quite some time."

"He'll help her. That husband of hers."

"Frankie, I told them both, many a time, Thank God on your knees for the love of a good man."

Then Hammond Mason came flying in, briefcase in one hand, tan jacket tailing out behind — he moved as fast as Apple. I felt his breeze, passing — "Evening, Frankie" — and then he kissed her face. Always put his arms around her and gave her a good kiss. She gave him as good back, and then he said, "Is that Apple in my bathroom?"

"Darling, she's been out riding, she needs to wash. We're having company. Did you see that Billy Long? Must be hanging around somewhere."

"Standing by his car in the drive. I asked him in. Apple just strand him?"

"We didn't think somehow to ask her where she'd left him."

"He's in the living room now, having a glass of sherry. Hot for sherry, but there's nothing else on the tray."

"Frankie, get that white wine out!"

I was dropping the potatoes in the popping water. "You want the new bottle?"

"Put it on a tray with some stem glasses and take it up to him. Sherry, this weather!" Mrs. Mason said.

I took the bottle and the glasses and went up.

Mr. Billy Long had not made himself comfortable. He was standing by the yellow damask curtains, looking out at the river. "It was silver a while ago," I told him, "but it's lost the light."

"Silver?" he asked me, playing for time. I put the wine down on the little round table.

"Mrs. Mason sent you this." Then I went back downstairs. Rosie, who's supposed to be my best friend, would have set him straight, right then: I raised Apple, she's my lap baby, knee baby, any gentleman come calling for her got to answer to me. I didn't plan to let him off that easy.

He stayed with me, going down the stairs — his face. Flat slab face I didn't think I'd seen before. Ordinary blue eyes. What was it, then? Hair like the inside of an oak leaf, where it's curled — that rich brown that's been protected from frost, black veined. Starting out of his head as though it was standing up with electricity, but soft, too, with a shine. I'd put my hand on that hair in a minute. Now what would an ordinary face like that do with that head of hair?

Below the neck I hadn't seen. He had on a blazer.

"Admit you don't really know him," she was saying when I came back. Then she turned to me. "He changed to the wine?"

"Looking at the river, hadn't touched his glass of sherry. I told him it was there."

"Poor wretch probably wonders where everybody is."

"I'll go up and keep him company," Mr. Mason said. "I was going to shower, but with Apple in my bathroom —"

"Goodness knows for how long!" She wanted him to deal with the guest.

"You know Billy's people?" she asked me, soon as he was gone. "What kind —?"

I racked my brain. "Seems to me Wilson was talking one time about a Mrs. Long, friend of Mrs. Peters. Mrs. Alberta Long, something like that."

"Sounds like a divorcée."

"No, I don't believe so. Believe she's a widow. People will lose track of a dead man's first name. Family's from around Bowling Green, some kind of connections there. Nice people." I was going out on a limb.

"What do you mean, nice?"

"I mean, plain. From the country. Solid."

"What kind of connections?"

"Wilson didn't say."

"How is Wilson, anyway?"

"Well, you know this hot weather is not the thing for his heart. And Mrs. Peters is on the go night and day. Wilson no more than gets the Buick in the garage than she's ringing for him to bring it out again. Had to put down his foot last week, tell her he needed a half day to wash and buff it, said he couldn't take her anywhere in the state that car was in. Won him a half a day, that's all, then ring! Ring! She wanted to go to her bridge game. It was Wednesday."

"How he takes that woman."

"Twenty-one years," I reminded her.

"I know, but — vulgar!"

"Just busy. What's Wilson going to do if she's not busy?"

"Nobody else has a chauffeur anymore."

"Guess we're lucky she does."

She finally saw my point. "Why, certainly, Frankie, in these times we all have to be grateful for a steady income." She was irritated, though: I hadn't said yes. She left to go change.

I threw in the broccoli. Those green trees upended, their trunks in the air, and I took a fork and fished up the flowerets. I started to melt the butter for my hollandaise sauce — she won't eat broccoli without it. I squeezed in my lemon, beat my eggs with a fork (she wants me to try that electric thing but I won't), and thought about Wilson coming home, about this time — our house on Grafton Street with the white stones he painted for an edge beside the sidewalks and the leggy petunias hanging out of the window box. Every week we have our Sunday together, work on that house like a pair of old fools, never even mention the fact that when we're gone, there isn't a soul in the world to take the place. It'll go to some trash; they'll root up my flowers, let a dog loose in Wilson's yard. He goes over it, Sundays, on his hands and knees, combing out every blade of crabgrass; and the no-accounts next door look out and spread their hands over their mouths, laughing at an old man that loves his grass.

There's a lot about Wilson I'd change if I had him to do again, but there's a lot I'd keep. He doesn't talk: she can't get over that. "Don't you talk when you eat?" she'll ask me. Usually we have the radio on. I don't mind him not talking; most of what people say is foolishness, anyway. Besides we're tired by the time Sunday comes. So we sit at the dinette table — it's a suite we got at Bacon's, four chairs and a table with a marbleized yellow plastic top — and when I get up to refill his plate, I listen to the scrape of the chair's metal feet on the floor. He laid the floor, squares of tile — wouldn't settle for linoleum. We've gotten to where we're just about surrounded by what we've made. I mean, my food, its smells — good food, too, the old kind but some of the new, as well: last Thursday, I made him fried shrimps — and his pictures on the wall, and the crooked-necked bridge lamp (from Mrs. Peters) with the crocheted shade I made, and the rug he hooked one winter when she was icebound and he was, too. Didn't have any shame about being seen with a bunch of bright red wool in his lap; said he's always wanted time to make a rug for that worn place in front of the sink. I said the rug was too good for that, but he didn't hear me. . . . Not hearing. . . . Not speaking. What kind of a man is that?

But soft in his ways, his silent ways. At night he reaches for my hand — we're laying side by side on our backs in the bed, listening to the radio music from next door (they're up all hours), watching car headlights shift cross the ceiling — and he reaches for my hand. Like we're just about to speak for the first time. Like it was the steps of the church, or a patch of sidewalk, or outside some decent place to eat instead of in our own big, hot bed, with the sheets I didn't get around to ironing. (He never would ask but I know what he likes.) Reaches for my hand and holds it, his big thumb in my palm. What more can you ask?

Kids, maybe. Yes, we could have had kids, back at the beginning, but what in the name would we have done with them? I didn't have a speck of family, or Wilson, either, except for his mother, who was too sickly to deal with babies.

I would have had to quit work, and that would've meant giving up the house — no way to keep up the payments — letting the furniture go, the dinette set, the sofa with the blue-and-green printed cover where you can see most of the fishes of the world, even our big bed. Going to live with my "family" (that's when they would have become my family), stuffed up in the cement room in the basement, hearing their feet over our heads.

So, no kids. Aside from that, it's been a good life.

Not that it's over yet. Not by a long shot. I've got years of work ahead of me.

When that busybody Rosie says to me, "How's your family?" standing on the church steps in one of her hats, I tell her, "He's fine. Had a little cold on his chest last week, but it went away."

She knows what I mean.

I stirred the hollandaise on the low burner — I'm beyond a double boiler — and as soon as it thickened, I poured it into her little brown-and-white sauceboat. It was golden.

CHAPTER FOUR

*M*R. MASON is sixty, I know for a fact — there's no way I could have worked for River City Hardware five years and not know it. Though where the fact came from, I couldn't say; it's not on any of the plaques in the office. Most of those honor his forefathers: G.M., who took the hardware firm on when it was declining in the depression and turned it into the biggest handler of gardening and construction supplies this side of the Mississippi; F.M., G.M.'s father (not much known about him), who inherited the firm before the turn of the century.

Mr. Mason didn't look his age, standing with the carving knife in one hand and the carving fork (do you call it that?) in the other, hovering over that chicken. Every gray hair in place, his face as shined as a waxed apple, concentration in his blue eyes: he slit the chicken breast neatly. The white meat peeled away from the sharp edge of the knife, and he turned to me and asked, "White or dark?"

"Dark," I said, remembering something my mother said once about taking what other people aren't likely to want.

He served my plate first. I couldn't get over the fact that I was being treated like a guest. Mrs. Mason put me on his right hand — and that's the place of honor, I know, the place I've wanted all my life — and sat herself next to me, and my girl went to her place directly across, sat down, and tapped my foot with her toe, under the table. Nothing amorous: it was a secret signal, something about being good and getting away early. I looked at Apple. She seemed to have grown younger since the riding, maybe because in the shower she'd washed her hair and it was still damp, curling around her face; Mrs. Mason, in fact, leaned over and shaped a few of those wisps around her finger. I didn't know Apple well enough to imagine the way she smelled, but those damp ringlets gave me a sense, a notion as though we were already intimate.

Their colored woman passed me a dish of broccoli and a bowl with some kind of yellow sauce in it; I assumed it was to go on the chicken. Apple told me to put it on the broccoli, and I swerved the spoon just in time. She did it in the right way, as though she was pointing out the only hard chocolate in one of those boxes where most of the chocolates have soft centers. I didn't mind.

"Were you raised here?" Mrs. Mason asked me in a nice way.

"Not here, but not too far away. My mother has the gatehouse on the old Wills estate." She looked at me, comprehending, and said, "I remember when Cora bought that place. I see her about every Sunday in church. She drives all the way out here for Steve Green's sermons! How are her petunias?"

"This dry spell hasn't done them any good. She's hoping for some rain."

"I do see a resemblance, around the eyes," Mrs. Mason said, peering at me. "Your mother has fine gray eyes. You're lucky to have inherited them!" I thought she might ask about my father's eyes, but she stopped in time.

"This young man's been working for me five years," Mr. Mason said. "Doing fine."

It was like being rolled in flour. I expected the hot oil next.

"You enjoy your work?" Mrs. Mason said, as though I had a choice of answers.

I couldn't very well explain that although I had never given a thought to a lifetime in hardware, it looked like about the best chance if I was going to stay in town. The firm had a reputation for bringing on its bright young men — there never had been any men in the Mason family except for the main one who ran the place, and he'd always, for three generations, had the sense to hire good helpers. I knew I would never get to the top, but I also knew they would let me rise to the next to the last stage. All the other family-owned businesses in town had uncles or cousins or nephews at that level, and outsiders didn't stand a chance.

"I started out clerking in the mail-order department, went on to accounting, then I spent a while in advertising. I liked that. Even learned something about layout and design. Right now, I'm assistant to Mr. Bergson —"

"It's a training job, " Mr. Mason quickly explained. "He won't be there long."

I wondered one more time about all the flour.

The colored woman — Frankie — came in again with the broccoli and the sauce, and this time I knew what to do with the sauce. I winked at Apple, but she had her eyes on her plate.

"Apple's not eating her dinner," Frankie said, passing behind her.

I guess I stared.

"Ate next to no lunch," she went on, "and now looks like she's going to get away with no dinner."

"What's wrong, darling?" Mrs. Mason asked, without a flicker of a look at Frankie.

"I lost my appetite," Apple grumbled.

"Honey, don't look like a thundercloud. We thought you were enjoying yourself," Mrs. Mason said.

"I *hate* all this talk," Apple said, glaring at me, tapping both my feet under the table.

"What talk?" her mother asked, smooth as cream.

"All this foolishness!"

Mrs. Mason said, "You know I don't permit impertinence at my dinner table."

"If I could find another word for it, I'd use it," Apple said, and I, for one, believed her. "Can't you all treat each other like human beings?"

"How do you know we aren't?" I asked her and added, under my breath, "Miss Scarlett!" I didn't know her well enough to know she was putting on something of an act, but I was close to guessing.

"You like it fine, I can tell that," she scolded me.

"Yes, I do," I said. "It's a privilege to have a chance to get to know your parents."

"Good Christ," she said and stood up, dropping her balled-up napkin in the middle of her plate.

"Adeline, Miss, you sit down," her father said.

"I'll go out to the kitchen with Frankie." Miss Apple took her plate and marched for the swinging door.

The colored woman barred her way. "No, you don't, Missie," she said. She was a big, solid figure of a woman, and Apple, in full career, stopped like she'd come up against a brick wall. "You sit right down and keep your guest company."

Apple came back like a lamb. I wondered if I needed to take a lesson from that woman. I never saw anybody look calmer than my girl. She picked up her knife and jabbed her napkin and threw it over her shoulder.

"Just don't pay any mind," Frankie said, looking hard at me, and then she went out to the kitchen.

They were broken to Apple's ways. They didn't say a word about that napkin — just went right on talking, pleased to have her back in her seat. I could see years and years of training ahead of me, and it bothered me and made me sad.

"I believe you know Corinne," Mrs. Mason said suddenly, as though she was trying to cheer me up. "Seems to me you came to her big party."

"I did. I remember this room. You had magnolia branches everywhere; it was like a grove."

She smiled. I had remembered the right detail. "That was a beautiful evening," she said. "The weather blessed us. And Corinne looked so pretty in that white dress."

Apple had to smile at that. She meant it to look mean, but she couldn't quite bring it off. "And spent the rest of the night throwing up in the bathroom," she said.

"Corinne always has had a sensitive stomach," Mr. Mason told me, as though he wanted to shield me from a shock. "She's older than Apple —"

"Five years," Apple said.

"But she's really the more —"

"Helpless?" Apple asked.

"Of course not!" Mrs. Mason cried.

"I was going to say, the more girlish of the two. Apple practically raised Corinne, not the other way around," Mr. Mason explained.

"Somebody had to fill the vacuum," Apple said.

"That was the year I was running for mayor, if I understand you correctly, Apple. Corinne was twelve and going through a hard time."

"Twelve, thirteen are the worst times for a girl," Mrs. Mason said.

"Apple was seven, and she watched over her big sister," Mr. Mason said.

"Has resented it ever since," Mrs. Mason said with a gentle smile.

"She'd have drowned herself in the river otherwise," Apple observed. Frankie was coming in and beginning to take away the plates. "Wouldn't Corinne have drowned herself in the river, that summer she was twelve, if I hadn't kept watch on her night and day?" Apple asked her.

Frankie stopped to think. She had a plate in each hand, and she stood balancing them like a statue of justice with eyes. "No, Miss Apple. I don't believe she would have. You wanted to think that, but I don't believe she would have. Miss Corinne always been crazy about *some things*," she added, "and that holds a person on to life."

61

"Some things is men," Apple translated for me.

"Corinne has been perfectly adequate with men since she was in kindergarten," Mrs. Mason said. "That's what they wrote on her first report card. Only of course then it was boys."

"She is certainly perfectly adequate now," Apple said, to start something else, and I was relieved when her father turned the tide with a question, to me, about a new kind of weed cutter he was thinking of carrying.

Frankie brought in a big bowl of custard for dessert and passed it first to me. I was serving myself when Apple said, "Look out for your finger bowl!" I looked down and saw this little glass bowl of water on my plate. "Just put it to one side," Mrs. Mason said soothingly. "Then later if you feel like it you can wash your fingers in it."

I moved the bowl out of the way and went at the custard again.

"You forgot the doily!" Apple said, and I looked down just in time to see a big spoonful of custard land on a round piece of lace.

"Now what do I do?" I asked her.

Frankie scooped my plate off and carried it out.

"I'm so sorry," Mrs. Mason said. "We cling to these old ways, and they do confuse people."

"The Prince of Wales once drank out of his finger bowl because one of his guests had," Mr. Mason remarked. I wondered if he had thought of dumping custard on his lace to spare me embarrassment.

Frankie came back with a fresh plate, and we started over. For some reason, the whole sequence reminded me of my first sex: trying to get things undone and off and out of the way, trying to get to the point of putting what I wanted in the right place. It'd seemed to me Laurie had as many hidden traps as a crystal bowl on a piece of lace on some kind of flowered plate: all ways to hold me back from what I wanted.

When I finally dug into the custard, it tasted fine.

"Apple and I are going to leave you two men down here to have your coffee," Mrs. Mason said when we'd finished eating, and she started for the stairs, sweeping Apple along in her wake. I knew my girl didn't exactly want to go, and I was grateful for Mrs. M's decisiveness.

Mr. Mason pushed back his chair and offered me several different drinks — I refused them all — and a cigar, which I accepted.

"How do you like our old-fashioned ways?" he asked me as soon as we lit up. He seemed to assume I might have a choice of answers.

"I've always believed in tradition, sir," I said. "My mother taught me that. 'You're never so poor you can't be clean,' she'd say."

He laughed. I hadn't meant it as a joke. "Sometimes I think my wife carries it too far. I mean, times change, habits change, customs change —"

"Not much else changes."

He thought awhile. "Well, I don't believe I can agree with you. For instance, when my father was running the company, he had three devoted friends who spent their lives helping him to make a success of it. I don't mean they sacrificed; they did well, too, had good lives. But their goal was to help him. You think I could find anyone like that, these days?"

"It would be harder. There's more of a scrambling mentality."

"That's what I see all around me," he said, leaning back till his chair creaked. "Scramblers."

I didn't say anything.

"Now if one of the girls had showed any kind of head for business . . ." He stopped. "I'm not saying I would have encouraged it. I don't think the women in a family ought to go beyond sitting on a board. They can come up with some fresh ideas. But let them into the business itself, the muck of it —" He shook his head. "No, I don't believe I'd have wanted either of the girls to come into it. Though I did have hopes, a long time ago, for Corinne."

"Yes?" I had caught the right tone; he did not hear my interest.

"That little girl was so bright." He sighed. "Taught herself to read when she was five years old, putting together headlines out of the newspaper. Could add and subtract before she went to school — big numbers: she used to work them out when she was playing outside. I'd hear her, under the magnolias. Of course she was quiet, the way bright girls tend to be; I can't speak for bright boys."

"My mother called me a slow starter."

He nodded. "The timetable seems to be different. Anyway, Cory won every prize they gave out at the Trinity School; the only awards she didn't win were the popularity ones — head of the class, all that. I mean, the other girls never could catch up with her, intellectually, and that caused some jealousy. Not that the intellect was what most of them aspired to! It was more getting picked up in a canary yellow Cadillac convertible on Fridays when school let out early."

"She do much of that?" I asked.

"Dating? Not a whole lot. You see, she had her mind elsewhere. She didn't make much of an effort. Her mother used to tell her, 'Sparkle! Sparkle, Cory!' That was her advice, when Cory first started to go to dances. Cory wouldn't do it, though. Her mother used to say she couldn't, but it wasn't that. She'd turned her energy elsewhere."

He paused, weighing his words, looking at the candle. It did not seem to strike him, yet, that I might consider it odd for him to spend our time together talking about his other daughter. Why he trusted me, I did not know, but the trust was gratifying.

"What happened to Corinne after school?" I asked.

"She got married," he said. "Eighteen years old, the summer before she was going East to college."

"That finished it?"

He did not answer me. "I like Buddy," he said. "He's a charming guy. Lawyer with one of the big firms. They live in New York.

"That leaves Apple," he said, in a different tone, grinding out his cigar. He stood up.

I stayed sitting, hoping to squeeze out a few more words. He turned away, expecting me to hop up and follow. "A different case," he said, and that was all.

How different? I wanted to ask, but knew better than to press. He was walking ahead of me up the stairs, his mind already elsewhere, the moment of confiding passed. A

65

different case? I wanted to ask him. How, a different case? Of course, I didn't know Apple well enough to make a reasoned comparison; but from what I knew of Cory, Apple had a better grasp on reality.

I went into the bathroom at the top of the stairs. "You know the house?" he asked when I came out.

"You were good enough to invite me to Corinne's deb party."

His face relaxed. "I'm surprised you remember. There are so many of those, every year; it seems to me there are more and more of them, all the time, even though you hear so many complaints about it costing too much. Still, every June, every September, and even in spring vacation, they sprout — those dinner dances, cocktail parties, teas. Apple won't have anything to do with it."

"I know."

"She tell you her reason?" His blue eyes danced with humor, and pride.

"She told me something about it being too exclusive."

"One little Jewish girl in her class at Trinity wasn't asked to be presented. That did it, for Apple. Not that the girl was any kind of special friend, but Apple, you know, has principles."

"She told me you always taught her to fight discrimination in all its forms."

"She say that?" He touched my arm, starting me along the hall.

"She admires you a great deal."

"That's good to hear," he said, expanding. "With your own children, you don't know."

66

"She's also very fond of you," I ventured, but that was going too far.

"Young man, I'm her father," he said, going ahead of me into the living room as though he was dismissing me. I followed. Mrs. Mason was sitting beside Apple on the sofa. As soon as she saw me, she reached for the silver coffeepot and called, "You take sugar? Two lumps?"

The rest of that part of the evening passed unprepossessingly enough. Apple was restless; she got up and down like a bird dog kept too long indoors; went to the window, looked out into the darkness, seemed to consider her reflection in the glass. Her parents were trying to keep me amused, but she didn't seem to care to help them. I almost wondered if she had a late date.

Finally, her mother stood up and excused herself, saying she had matters to attend to at her desk. When she gave me her hand, I felt its coolness and imagined smelling it: soap, Elizabeth Arden. She glanced at me, sharply. I wondered if she was starting to take me seriously already. The smoothness of her departure reminded me that this was a familiar routine, for them: Apple had been surrounded by men since she was fourteen years old. Her parents must have become resigned to seeing quite a few of us singed in the flame, crawling away crippled, leaving behind that dry burning smell. Mrs. Mason was probably only checking to see whether or not I was going to be able to crawl away.

They must dread midnight phone calls, I thought, unexpected visitations. I would have liked to reassure them, as a matter of pride.

Mr. Mason stayed on longer, more out of curiosity than

desire, I thought. We had a standard conversation about the hardware company in which he seemed to be giving me an opportunity to air complaints. I knew better than to take that offer. Anything I said would be seen in a different light, the following morning.

Finally he stood up with a big yawn and said he was heading for his bedroom. I noticed that he did not bother to invent an excuse, although it was only ten o'clock. He took out the coffee tray but left the liquor, telling me to get myself another drink if I should be so inclined.

Apple was at the window. He went to her and kissed the back of her blond head.

"Well, honey," he said. That was all. She did not turn around.

"Good night, Daddy."

As he left, he did not give me the judging look, and I almost believed he had learned enough about me, during dinner, to dispense with the formalities. I knew I'd shown well.

I let Apple stand for a while after they were gone. Her put-on restlessness had little effect on me. I poured myself another glass of her father's top-notch bourbon and sat down again on the silk sofa.

"Aren't you going to kiss me?" she asked, after a long silence. "Haven't you been waiting for that, all evening?" I heard her father's voice: the mixture of humor and pride.

"No, I don't believe I will. At least, not right now. I'm enjoying my drink. I'm enjoying sitting here on this silk sofa. It is silk, isn't it?" When she didn't answer, I went on, "I had an interesting conversation with your father after dinner."

That made her turn around. "About me?"

"No. He talked mostly about your sister."

"Daddy's always been soft on Cory," she said, without bitterness. "Of course, she was so bright."

"I haven't noticed that you lack anything in that department."

"Oh, me!"

"You're close to Corinne?"

"Not so much anymore. We don't see each other. She's in New York, only comes down here to visit once or twice a year, and then there's so much family . . ." Suddenly, she asked, "You know Corinne, already, don't you?"

"I met her at a few parties, before she got married."

There was a pause. Apple came and sat down near me on the sofa. She folded her hands on her knee and jiggled her foot, dropping her gold sandal off her heel. I admired her ankle. She said, "You want to mystify me, don't you?"

"Not particularly."

"I thought the first time I saw you, leading that horse: there's one that will mystify me."

"That's not really what I intend."

"What do you intend, then?" she asked, mocking my solemnity, and she laid her hand, palm up, on my knee.

I looked at that pink palm. She was provoking. I didn't know yet whether it was a trait that needed to be weeded out.

"I haven't decided," I told her. "I hope we can be friends."

"How boring!" She borrowed her mother's voice, for a change: that trill.

"What do you want?" I asked her sharply, knowing only too well what she was going to reply.

69

"Oh, just to enjoy myself," she said and sighed as though she was oppressed by the weight of the world. "You'd be amazed how hard that is."

"Really? I would have thought, when it's your sole occupation —"

"Everyone's so terribly boring!"

"Boring is a boring word. If you'll forgive me, I've found the only bored people are the ones who don't take an interest in anything outside of themselves."

"Is that what I am?" She leaned forward to look at me. "Selfish?"

"You haven't been raised to be anything else."

"Oh, I can't blame them" — she sighed — "because they've always given me everything I ever wanted."

"That seems to mean you don't want anything anymore."

"Yes," she said. "That's it. I don't understand it. There's that line in *Hamlet*: appetite grows with what it feeds on. I think a lot about that. It's not true. Appetite gets dulled. It stops. Nothing is worth wanting anymore. Why, yesterday" — and she picked up her false sparkle — "some boy sent me a camellia corsage, out of nowhere! I mean, he wasn't taking me to a dance, or anything. I remember when the sight, just the sight, of the florist's truck would make my heart beat. When Frankie handed me the box, I couldn't even bring myself to open it. I got her to open it. 'Why, smell this beautiful flower,' Frankie told me. I didn't even want to smell it . . ."

"I promise never to send you flowers," I said, standing up.

"You're leaving?" She looked up at me pathetically, as

though she was at the bottom of a well. "It's so early. I never go to bed before midnight."

"You forget I'm a working man. I have to be up before seven."

She followed me to the door. "I don't believe you've enjoyed yourself," she said, softly.

I knew that for what it was, and I answered, without turning around, "I don't want to disappoint you, but I've enjoyed myself a great deal."

She opened the door for me — the first time, but not, I was prepared to swear, the last. It had begun to rain, blades falling through the yellow beam from the porch light. She held out her hand, palm up — "You'll get soaked" — and held out her mouth as though it was on a tray. She also closed her eyes.

By the time she opened them, I was in my car. I heard her yelp. Then she slammed the front door. It didn't matter. I'd given her something to sleep on. We won't have, I was ready to tell her, any prepared kisses.

CHAPTER FIVE

I WENT ON HOME.

They were waiting up for me, one light on in the living room and both of them sitting under it.

"Deadbeat," my sister said, like she was talking about herself, shoes off, her uniform stained across the front as though she'd been cooking spaghetti instead of hooking up bodies to IV's.

Mom said, "I suppose so," talking in code the way they do.

"It's not even eleven," I told them, then wished I didn't sound so put-upon. "What did you all have to eat?"

Mom sighed, moving her feet to one side of the hassock to show me where to sit. "That liver."

"We knew you'd be glad to miss it," my sister said, "after that hell you raised this morning."

I sat by my mother's feet, wearing those big hairy bedroom slippers. "I don't want to have to decide at eight o'clock in the morning what I'm going to eat at six o'clock that night."

"And didn't come home anyway," my mother said.

"I called you."

"Yes, I know, I don't have a thing to complain about," she said, looking up at me with those washed gray eyes. She was a pretty lady — I have a picture on my bureau — but scraping all these years to make the payments on the gatehouse (that's what we all call it, though the main house, if there ever was one, is long gone) has taken her looks.

I told her once I didn't need to live in the suburbs; the frame house Dad left us in the old part of downtown was fine by me. I always knew I was going to have to make it on my own. But the good public schools were in the suburbs, as well as what Mom calls exposure, and she wanted us to have all that: birthday parties, later square dances, National Merit scholarships, finally a deb party or two. They scrape you off fast enough, but along the way you learn. For years Mom thought my sister was going to marry, and the gatehouse, small as it is, has a flight of stairs she wanted to see her come down in a long white dress.

"How are the Masons?" my sister asked.

"Fine."

Mom let out a sigh. "Now, I want to hear. What did they have to eat?"

"I don't remember. I wasn't concentrating on the food."

"At least say what flowers, and what color the mats were," my sister pleaded. "They must have had candles."

"Wine with dinner, or just drinks beforehand?" Mom wanted to know.

"Hold on a minute. I don't remember any flowers except some Mrs. Mason was arranging in the hall."

"I read they're not putting flowers on the table now because they interfere with people talking," Mom said. "What about the conversation?"

"Mrs. Mason remembered your petunias," I said, hoping it would make her smile, and it did.

"My land, that's been years ago."

"Was that when you used to see her at church?" my sister asked, leaning forward.

"Yes, indeed, it was, and I've always wondered why she stopped coming, though I did hear they go to that new church out by the river," my mother said. She went on for a while about what Mrs. Mason used to wear at each season of the year and how at times it seemed she'd planned her outfit to complement the altar hangings.

"Is that why you liked her?" I asked; I still felt spiteful about all those Sunday washed ears and button-down collars. Mom finally quit trying when I turned twenty-one.

"You may not understand this, young man, but she was kind to me," my mother said. I could have broken down and cried. "That's part of church teachings, too. A lot of people out here go to that new church by the river, I know that," Mom went on as though she'd been challenged, "but I just can't seem to abandon Reverend Dorsey downtown." When she talked like that I remembered her graduation photograph in the Presentation Academy yearbook, perched to fly off into world.

"Monkey see, monkey do," Sis said, sitting back and looking at her nails.

"Well, you do meet younger people in the new church; they have picnics and so on," my mother began, but Sis held up her hand.

"You don't need to switch churches so I can meet people."

"I didn't mean it that way, honey," Mom said, and I wondered when she got so humble. "It's just if you take Billy for an example —"

"Some example!" Sis was laughing, but she meant it.

"He never would have met Mr. Mason if he hadn't worked that summer caddying at the country club."

"My own kind of Rhodes Scholarship," I said, but they didn't get it.

"I don't know what the country club has to do with church," Sis said. "I have more male companionship than I can put up with at the hospital, anyway." She's five years older than me, and the long hours at work are starting to show, although when she starts out in the morning she can look fresh. She's proud of her degree and the little peaked hat she gets to wear, to go with it, but it looks like she's gone about as far up the ladder as she can with the Baptists.

"I just want you to be happy," Mom said, to both of us. "That's the reason I go on out here. It was up to me I'd move back down to Third Street, walking distance from the library. I've been happy in my life, though it didn't last. That's all I want for you two. It doesn't seem like a lot to ask."

I wanted to ask her when she was happy, but I was afraid she would say it was now.

"I'm happy enough, and Billy has his parties," Sis said.

"I don't believe he's been to a real party since Cory Mason's debut, and that was years ago," Mom said. Then she launched into the story of Cory's debut, or that part of it she knew about from the Sunday society section, which had

75

run a long article, with pictures. "Of course I couldn't tell from the black-and-white, but it looked like to me her dress was either pink or pale gray, with flounces."

I said, "It was pink."

"And here you don't remember what you ate for dinner," my sister said.

"Dresses and dinner are different."

"That's so," Mom said. "You were always sensitive to colors, even when you were little."

My sister was speculating. "That was about the last year Cory was here, wasn't it? Seems to me I read the story about her wedding that fall."

"Yes, she was supposed to go to college somewhere in the East, but she got married instead," Mom said, looking at me. "I wonder was that a mistake."

"Nobody talks much about her, out there," I said.

"I wonder why not." Mom's learned to be cautious.

"I don't think there's much communication, or at least that's the way Apple tells it. No big break or anything but just kind of drifting apart." As I said it, I sensed Apple's sadness and wondered what use it would be.

"You came back after that party of Cory's and wouldn't say a word," my sister said.

"You were tied up with Marvin, you wouldn't have heard a word," I said, hoping to run her off the track, but she just laughed.

"Oh him, that was never serious, just someone to go to the movies with. But I think you had something in mind, with Cory."

"I don't know where you got that." We've gone on this

way since we were kids, wrangling over a peppermint stick.

"I expect you made a mess of things," my sister said. "That is if you had the chance."

"Hush," Mom said. "It's late. I don't want you two fighting."

"You're thinking about Marvin and how he messed you up," I said. "I've got to go to bed."

In the doorway I looked back at them. They were leaning towards each other in that patch of light, and I knew what they would look like in twenty years: two bookends.

It wasn't so much that Mom couldn't face living alone — she did pretty well after Dad pulled out — but my sister needs to hear her stories. Mom has a way of making sense of things, fitting everything into a box. I could hear her starting: "That Marvin always reminded me of my cousin Tom, well, he isn't a cousin, really, but his father was somebody my grandfather had a lot of respect for —" She'd go on as long as my sister was willing to listen.

Sis doesn't have any stories except about the things that happen in the hospital, and after a few years of that, Mom asked her to quit bringing it home. I expect good things go on in the hospital, too, but Sis has an eye for evil.

That leaves her without any stories to tell.

In the attic, I went behind my curtain and pulled it close to the wall, pinning it with a chair. It didn't do anything to preserve my privacy, but I liked to pretend it did. I was about to begin having stories, and the last thing I wanted was to shout something in the night. I do that sometimes, talk in my sleep.

I hung up my suit and lay down in bed in my underwear,

too tired to fool with pajamas. I looked at my legs and decided I'd have to get out in the sun on Saturday, mow the grass, start turning a healthier shade. I didn't need exercise; running from floor to floor in the warehouse — I avoided the old elevator — took care of that; but I was white like all indoor-working, hard-pressed people, and I remembered Apple's skin, that rosy tan. She didn't burn or peel, she took on a sort of glow, and I knew she probably worked on it, as the girls said, for a certain amount of time every day.

The air was thick and hot; we slept in a storage space, not intended for human habitation; when we first looked at it, there were pigeons in the rafters. I could smell pigeons, in that heat. Mom and Sis painted the walls and made curtains and did the best they could with what sticks of furniture we had from in town, but the place was still an attic. My room — as they called it — is a section curtained off at the end; they sleep in the one room that has real walls.

I told Mom if she'd left the downstairs alone instead of putting up wallpaper and buying a sofa and two lamps, there would have been money enough to make me a wall, but she reminded me the downstairs is the part of the house company sees. I didn't have the heart to ask her what company; after Marvin stopped coming by to pick up Sis, the only visitor was Mrs. Ash from church, with her complaints. Mom always has a ready ear.

After a while I heard them coming up the stairs, tiptoeing, their shoes in their hands. Mom was still talking, and I caught a few words about what she would need to get in the morning for dinner. I knew at breakfast she'd look down at the table and ask me, as quietly as she could, what I'd want to eat, and if I wasn't careful, I'd snap. I didn't mean to be short with her, but when she made her plans, I felt like she'd thrown a rope around my neck and was pulling it tight.

I knew they were undressing in stages, hanging their dresses on the hooks behind the door and laying their underwear out on the chair, to air. They have their ways, so matched now it's hard to believe there was a time, not too many years ago, when Sis screamed at Mom and spent the night downstairs on the new sofa.

I'd told myself I wasn't going to dream — I told myself that every night — so I wouldn't run the risk of waking them, but dreams are not easy to control. Probably it was the heat, or the excitement of that evening at the Masons', but I woke up way late in the night with words coming out of my mouth and Mom standing by the curtain in her bathrobe. "You were shouting," she said, and I didn't dare to ask what she'd heard; I turned over and put my face in the pillow. I swore I'd get something, a gag, if I had to, to put in my mouth at night. "What happened?" she wanted to know.

What happened, I said into the pillow, willing her to go back to bed, is life. Just plain old life that had to be lived, gone after, on my own terms, and there was nothing she, or Sis, could do to help me or harm me. I was on my way like a leaf on a current — she might understand, if I put it that way.

I heard her slip away, padding back to her bed. Sis was up, too, and I heard her ask what was wrong. "He's worried about something," Mom said, and I was relieved to hear how far off the mark she was. That's all I have, for privacy: the fact that I've moved on, a few inches anyhow, and they don't know it.

Falling back to sleep, I wondered how Apple would cope with them, what she'd find to say. It didn't matter a lot, but it would make my life easier if she found some kindness for them. I didn't really consider them my family, I couldn't afford to; they seemed more like a pair I'd picked up hitch-hiking. Maybe Apple could understand them that way: they were still mine, but I wasn't theirs, not anymore.

CHAPTER SIX

ORINNE, a blond girl, twenty-five, seven years married, sat at her desk in New York and started a letter to her
parents. She wrote to them regularly, once a week, since
they shared a dread of the telephone.

"Appearances are deceiving," she had told Buddy the
evening before over the last of her last crepes suzette. "I am
through with cooking." She was also coming to the end of
writing letters and had not progressed beyond the "dear
Mommy and dear Daddy," which embarrassed her but
which she did not know how to change.

"Is today the fifth or the sixth?" she called through the
open door to Buddy, who was down on his knees in the
hall, fiddling with the stereo speakers. Buddy liked to have
the music on to greet guests; he was looking to be made a
partner in his law firm, and their entertaining required a
special flavor. "Those were my last crepes," she added,
under her breath.

"The sixth," he said. "Did you order the leg of lamb?"

"Lamb's gone up so —"

"It's one thing that's sure to be good."

"I've cooked my last crepes," she said, out loud.

After a while, he said, "I'll get some of those French apricot tarts, from the pastry shop."

"That'll be the first time we've ever had an outside dessert."

"Remember to fix the flageolets the way Mimi Sheraton did them in *The Times*."

"I don't like beans, I like new potatoes."

"But we're doing the lamb the French way, pink in the middle, and that goes with flageolets and garlic." The speaker gave a loud whine and was abruptly silenced. "Corinne?" he asked, after a while.

"I'm writing my parents."

"Oh yes, the weekly letter. Don't go into everything, will you?"

They talked best across distance, when they could not see the shadows which sailed over each other's faces, disrupting their twinned, calm look; they were still mistaken for brother and sister. At their best, they put their best feet forward for the attorneys and their pretty wives whose favors Buddy needed; Corinne, in her long gowns, laid on her southern accent, and the guests found her charming although somewhat enigmatic. Afterwards Buddy would wash up while she lay with her feet up and her shoes off on the couch, and then usually they would make love.

"Everything?" she asked innocently, looking out at the great park which lay swimming in green beneath the library windows.

"The doctors. They won't want to know. Your mother will feel harassed."

Corinne turned to stare at the open doorway as though Buddy might put his head in. That would have silenced them both. "I don't really have anything to write about all that. Dr. Stewart says he can't tell anything till the tests come back."

"Well then don't raise it."

Corinne idled her pen across scratch paper, making big and small loops. She wondered what her mother would have thought about the decoration of the waiting room at Dr. Stewart's: too much green and yellow, in vibrant, unrelenting hues, and a crowd of small furniture for the large women to gather on. They did not speak to each other, although there were many surreptitious glances. Corinne was always surprised by the scarcity of pregnant women in Dr. Stewart's antechamber; it dismayed her to realize that the troubles of the reproductive system were more widely represented there than its successes. She longed to see a bustling pregnant lady in a navy blue two-piece costume with a white collar.

"When will he get the tests back?" Buddy asked, from the hall. He had finished with one speaker and was working on the other.

"He said next week sometime." She went on with the conversation in her head. Does it matter, Buddy? If he says we can't? Of course it doesn't matter, darling. I love you for you, you know that. Would you consider another way to do it if it turns out you are the one who can't? (But that's so unlikely: men always can — you can see them doing it every

83

night of the week, up and away; whereas with women it is secret, hidden, more likely to go wrong: "Like a closed reel — the line's always getting fouled," Buddy had said. Fishing was his only occupation outside of the law and even fishing had fallen off since no one at the firm was interested in going with him.) How have I gotten this far? Corinne wondered, closing the parenthesis in her mind, and returned to the singsong question, sweetened almost out of meaning: Does it matter, Buddy? Does it matter?

She was tormented sometimes in her daily routine, her exercise class, her shopping, her walks in the park, by a sense of inconsequence. The year before, she had narrowly escaped being hit by a taxi at the corner of Eighty-fifth and Park, and after that the idea of inconsequence had rooted and flowered.

"Without babies, we will die," she said to Buddy, in the hall, and listened for a while to his silence. Then she went on, "We are spoiled rotten like the children of the rich, given everything. We have everything we want. I can come home with the world on my back — silk from India, gold from Chile, I don't know." She was running on senselessly as she always did when he did not reply, embroidering the silence between them, making it beautiful.

"We will not die," he said firmly. "You mustn't believe that. If we can't have babies, we'll find something else."

She laughed. Young energy overcame her, and she bounded up from the chair. She darted out into the hall and saw him sitting back on his heels, looking up at her from under the edge of the console table. As she leaned down to kiss the top of his head, she dropped her hand on the marble. It was cool, as always. "When I come in and lay my purse down here, I always feel the marble," she told him as he turned up his face and gave her a kiss back. "When the apartment is so quiet, the marble seems like an echo. We have a marble table in the front hall at home."

"Do you need to go see your mother?"

"Not necessarily. I should have learned by this time to put up with things here." He did not tell her that was the thing for her to do, so she went on, a spasm of impatience contorting her smooth, clear voice. "You know, I didn't wait yesterday at Dr. Stewart's. I was embarrassed to tell you, when I came home. I sat for an hour, I read all the old magazines — the room was so hot and smelly and crowded. Finally I stood up and left."

"What did the nurse say?"

"I went out when her back was turned. I was afraid she'd shout after me. She didn't even have the decency to telephone, find out if I'd died, or what. Just crossed me off the list, I guess! At home Dr. Maddox used to come all the way out to the house to see us when we had colds. I'd hear his car horn round the bend —"

"That'd be easier, wouldn't it?"

"At home they all know who you are."

"You want to go to a doctor down there?"

"I guess I've burned my bridges," she said, and then was frightened. "No, not yet. I don't want to go down there in hot weather, it's too uncomfortable. I'll wait till winter."

"What about the tests?"

"I guess they'll call me when they get the results." She was near asking him whether it mattered — his fair face was so close — but he stood up and went to put his tools away. Standing forlorn, she thought he might notice her — a barren lady, her empty arms hanging slightly curved by her sides. He did not look back.

In the kitchen, he called her. "Where's the roaster? Have you checked to see if it's clean?"

Like two children exploring a cave, they got down on their knees to search the kitchen cabinet. The roaster clanked out, bright under a coating of grease. "Doesn't Mary get to these cabinets at all?"

"She doesn't like to kneel down," Corinne said. It was hard to explain to Buddy that Mary had to do as she pleased. On Tuesdays, when she came to clean, Corinne put on a dress instead of slacks and they shared tuna fish sandwiches and fresh fruit for lunch.

"I'll scrub it," Buddy said without resentment, and Corinne watched him roll up the sleeves of his fine blue shirt.

"You don't have to do that now," she said. "It's only two o'clock."

"A leg of lamb is going to take a while to roast, even just till it's pink."

"But I didn't get a leg of lamb — I told you. It's too high."

He turned to her with the first hint of an expression. "What did you get?"

"Lamb shoulder, cut up for stew. There's a recipe in *The New York Times Cook Book*."

It had been a long time since he had looked at her with dismay. It sharpened his features, pointed his nose; his face impressed itself on her drifting attention. She found herself staring at him, fumbling behind her for the cookbook, which lay on the counter. "It's a good French country recipe."

"I told Claude we'd be having leg of lamb. It happens to be his favorite."

This was the senior partner for whom Buddy had bought a silver goblet at Christmas. At the time, Corinne had thought he was going too far. However, a thank-you note had arrived and an invitation to dinner, which had proved Corinne silly and wrong.

"Shall I call him up and tell him we're reduced to stew?"

"No, never mind. He's probably forgotten anyway."

How awful his depression was. Now he would sag all afternoon.

To stir him out of it, Corinne said, "I haven't shined the silver, either. I thought we'd use the stainless."

"Well, I guess I've got time." With humble bent back, he fished under the sink for the polish.

Oh God, Corinne fumed. If I can't make him angry, I'll kill him. It was so new a thought that she wondered at its freshness and vigor, at her imagination which was still able to bring forth such a flower. She thought of putting a little paring knife to his throat and slitting him down as far as she could reach into his French collar. Her fingers clutched. How he would bleed and stare.

"Corinne, there isn't a single rag under here," he said. "What does Mary do with them?"

"I take them and rinse them out when she's finished." Corinne went to the drying rack and took off the rags. "Here's a nice pink one, made out of a pair of my underpants."

He took the pink square, knotted it up, and dabbed it into the silver polish. Then he began, with long strokes, to lay it on the handles of the knives.

Corinne hovered. She thought of taking a walk in the park. She thought of the feel and taste of the damp spring air, the last dash and savor of it before she came in to cook. She thought of leaving the whole dinner to him — coming in late, flushed, like a woman hurrying home from a job or an important meeting, full of flustered apologies.

"I'm going out for a walk," she said.

"That's an excellent idea. Fresh air. We've been inside all day.

As she turned away, she thought of asking him to go with her and decided against it.

She buttoned up the tan jacket her mother had given her. Her mother's carefulness hung in it, in the buttons sewn on with double thread and the knotted loop inside the collar. Of course Frankie had added that, but it had been Mrs. Mason who paid.

"I have been so happy since I have been married," she said in the hall, shaping the words to pierce the dense air.

"I am so glad, darling. I thought you'd been looking distracted lately," Buddy said from the kitchen.

She went out. It was an East Side apartment building, very much comme il faut, as Mrs. Mason had said, with a series of smiling elevator men, a stained white awning, and a light to call cabs. It reminded Corinne of the dollhouse her mother had passed on to her; every detail in place, a feat of active re-creation. She was pleased that the flowers in the front hall were real and that no one ever saw who put them there: daisies, today, an incongruously simple touch against the brocade panels and stiff green upholstered chairs.

"Good morning," she said to Michael, the wiry Irishman, and wondered why none of the elevator men was ever attractive.

She crossed the street and went into the park, where the playground was full of Saturday parents. The children circled in bands or alone from the big sandbox to the crippled sliding board and the fenced-in bank of swings; the parents sat on the benches, chatting. Corinne stopped to watch them. She remembered a monkey at the Cincinnati Zoo, years ago, hanging on his bars to watch the passersby; she too would have liked to hang on the high wire mesh fence around the playground, peering in.

The path ribboned on to a worn green meadow, patched here and there with bare dirt. A lot of dogs were cavorting, and Corinne stopped to stare at them, too. How freely they ran . . . a big German shepherd, some lady's poodle, a pair of retrievers; how their dissimilarities seemed to melt away as they chased, galloping, across the city meadow. Their owners, leashes in their hands, stood talking at the edge of the grass. Corinne, too, had thought about getting a dog, but she did not want to be obliged to get up in the morning and walk it. Her day's pleasure came when she stayed in the warm bed after Buddy left for work.

When her mother was unbuttoning the sixty satin-covered buttons on the back of her wedding dress, seven years ago, she had said, "Now, Corinne, darling — no more excuses." The sentence came back, now and then, enigmatic, challenging. Corinne, walking through the city meadow, thought of it again and wondered what excuses her mother meant.

Her mother had raised her according to a strict and special rule. She was kept close at hand as a young girl, dressed simply, even severely, fed a diet of protein and leafy green vegetables, exercised daily, read to at night. Looking back, she remembered herself as a pallid, grave little girl, the uncertain result of such certain experiments. Physically, at least, they had been remarkably successful; she had a purity of line, which seemed, to her own eyes, more closely akin to the grace of a perfectly bred dog than to a human's muddled charm. Her mother had raised her to please — but more than that: to be a perfect example of the woman who in pleasing the world, ultimately, secretly, shamelessly pleases herself.

At that, Corinne felt a spasm of intense unhappiness, a physical knotting up. She stopped in her tracks. It was the old hard knot of helplessness, twisting tighter and tighter. She still felt herself raised, trained, unable to escape the development of her own perfection.

In bed — she had hoped — it would go: let him get at the knot and jerk it loose. Buddy, however, admired her, cherished her for the qualities her mother had planted for him to cherish. Sometimes at dinner parties, Corinne would hear him bragging about her, how she was the prettiest, the gentlest, the best-tempered . . . Then the knot would tighten.

She turned into a smaller path, which led off to a grove of ginkgoes. The grass was long and fine here, brilliantly green, like the uncropped grass at the edge of a cow pasture. It was difficult to believe that this was city grass and city air. The path was cracked; an old water fountain trickled a puddle along one side. Downhill, she saw the highway which ran through the park and heard the whine of cars. The tennis courts were ahead. In between, a thick green grove of ginkgoes fluttered their fan-shaped leaves.

Oh beautiful city, she thought, and gave a skip, like a rabbit's. Then she walked into the dappled shade.

Almost at once, she saw two young men sitting on a rock, half-naked in a patch of sun. They were turned on their sides, facing each other, their bare feet intertwined. It's the Wild Wood, she thought, remembering the drawing of Mole venturing alone into darkness and trees in *The Wind in the Willows*. She passed rapidly by the pair, who did not move, did not even sense her presence. On a bench farther along, a young man with long blond curls sat staring at his hands. He looked up sharply as she approached and as sharply looked down again. Corinne had felt the lash of that look before — New York was not a city for women who longed to be appreciated; this time, however, her humor rose instead of her anger, and she stopped in front of the young man.

"You look like you don't want me to be here," she said.

He looked up, startled. His skin was very pale, and there were premature lines around his soft mouth. His hair fell forward on either side of his jaw. When he spoke, it was with a midwestern twang: "Didn't see you at all," he said.

She laughed. The sound, in that stillness, was explosive. He looked up at her again. She wanted to howl like a wild thing. "Don't you see," she gasped, "it's so silly — here I am in my expensive dress and my high heels and my stockings and here you are in your old corduroy pants and that sweater —"

"Look, lady, I just came here to sit down."

"Can I sit down with you?" He scuttled sideways on the bench, and she perched herself at the end, crossing her legs and drawing one ankle close to the other. "You see, we can be comfortable together," she said. "There's no wall holding us apart, is there? What's your name?"

He turned to stare at her, and she saw that he still had a few of his adolescent pimples. "Freddie, with an -ie," he said.

"That's a nice name. That sounds like the South. You come here a lot?"

"Indiana," he said. "Yes."

"Why, that's across the Ohio from where I came from!"

"Really? You don't sound like a southerner."

"I've gotten over a lot of it since I've been living in New York."

"How long?"

"Seven years," she said and sighed, heavily.

"You like it?"

"I don't have much choice," she said. "I'm married, he works here — you know."

"How'd a girl from the South" — and she heard the relief it was for him to drop into the formula — "how'd a girl from the South get herself carried all the way up here?"

"My parents used to take us abroad every summer, and Buddy was on the boat."

"How romantic!" Again, she recognized his pleasure at being able to lock the formula into place.

"Buddy danced with me once, after supper, and I thought that was the end of it. I mean, he hardly even asked my name. You get so used to boys coming and going, always looking for something else, somebody else, over your shoulder on the dance floor or whatever. Or else they want to be simply physical, as my mother called it, and of course that doesn't work at all."

"No?"

"No," she said firmly. "So when the next morning there were flowers outside my door, a regular bouquet with a note, I was flabbergasted. I mean, the decision, the planning. Thinking of something to write on the note. You know what I mean? Picking up the telephone and ordering the flowers, deciding which ones, how many, paying. It seemed so amazing to me. To decide."

"So you married him."

"Well, not just like that. Of course not just like that!" She was amused. "But he came right on down to visit me as soon as we got home; he called me on the telephone every other day; he wrote me on the days he didn't telephone — short notes, but good. I caught my father one time studying his handwriting, when I'd left an envelope lying on the hall table: "Very mature, I like his *m*'s." Well, there were all these things going on at the time. I was fighting with my mother and . . . Why am I telling you all this?"

"I don't know, but I like it." He inched a little closer to her. "Was it a great big wedding?"

"Huge." She found nothing more to say.

"Tents, and champagne, and caviar?"

"It was too hot for caviar. It was July. Mother said, 'What possesses you to get married in this heat?' I was trying to get things settled as fast as I could so I could start to make some decisions of my own. I mean, where we would live. What the dining room table would look like — all those things. I never had made small decisions, because there were rules for everything and everything was decided ahead of time. You ever feel a knot around you? Like a knot in a rope? Rubbing and grinding against your skin? That's the way I felt, all the time, at home — I mean, after I got to be ten or eleven. I wanted the chance to make some decisions for myself, and I knew Buddy would let me do that. Or I thought he would."

"Did he?"

"Well, it got confusing. You see, he already had his life mapped out. I wanted an apartment down in the Village, where the trees are so pretty and there's so much going on in the streets, but Buddy felt it wouldn't be appropriate. He's an attorney. He thought we ought to get ourselves settled somewhere convenient where we could entertain. That's about all we've been doing, the last seven years. Of course, it'll get better when he's made a partner. I mean, we'll be able to relax."

"So what do you do with yourself?" he asked, taking out a crumpled cigarette and lighting it.

"Every day in every way I get better and better."

"That sounds all right."

She didn't want to talk to him anymore. He was relaxing, starting to smoke, ready to take up his part of the conversation. She was sure he would have a lot to describe — how he'd escaped Indiana, in spite of his parents, how he was making it or not making it in New York. She stood up abruptly. "I don't know what came over me. I guess I needed to talk. Thanks, Freddie —"

"You don't really need to know my name."

"Well, I guess that's right. Still, thanks for letting me sit with you."

She left him with a hard glance she thought would last him awhile.

The light was beginning to fail. She pushed on farther through the ginkgoes and came out on a bare slope leading down to the tennis courts. Bathed in sun, a small mob of white-clothed people were surging back and forth across the green cement. From the distance, the tennis players seemed to be a confused army, sallying abruptly off in various directions.

The tennis courts were surrounded by a high mesh fence. Cutting across the grass, Corinne went to the fence and stood close to it, looking through. After a while, she hooked her fingers in the mesh and pressed still closer. It delighted her to see people so involved in the work at hand. No one had even turned to see her, watching.

She ran her eyes around the periphery of the tennis courts. There were about thirty, nearly all of them in use. As she moved her eyes along the fence, she saw a tall black man standing about five courts away from her. He, too, was watching the tennis, his long dark hands hooked in the mesh. After a while, he turned his head and looked at her.

Corinne began to make her way along the fence towards

him. She passed a large woman on one court, and a pair of teenagers who were laughing and chiding each other. The next court was empty, and she passed it swiftly, hand over hand on the wire. The black man watched her move onto the edge of his court. She stopped ten feet away from him and hooked her hands in the fence. Without looking, she knew he had slowly turned back to the game.

Two young women in white tennis dresses were batting the ball back and forth on the court. They began after a time to hit hard, and to run, and their white skirts flew up over their buttocks. Corinne, looking sideways, saw the man lay one of his hands on his fly.

She turned back and looked at the two women. Down the fence, she heard a soft sobbing sound, which grew in intensity as the minutes passed. She thought it was an electrical sound, like the buzz from a big generator: soft, almost inaudible. She kept her eyes fixed on the woman who was serving.

The woman double-faulted and turned suddenly to the fence. "Get away from here, you filthy bastard!" she shrieked.

The black man turned and skidded off, and at the same time, Corinne turned in the opposite direction and ran away on light feet.

Coming into the apartment, she smelled the lamb and heard the tinkle of voices in the living room. The air was hot and stale. She took off her jacket, dropped it on the chair, and called from the hall, "I'll be right with you."

CHAPTER SEVEN

CLAUDE HUGHES, Buddy's senior partner, had invited them to the Wildwood Club for supper; it was June, a Saturday night, six months after Corinne and Buddy started spending weekends in the country. Claude told Buddy to tell Corinne not to dress, which made Corinne laugh. She went to take a shower at six, put her hair up with a multitude of pins, and asked Buddy what he thought about her wearing the orange chiffon.

"Much too dressy, this is the country," he said, rather sharply.

"But these are all New York people, transplanted to Dutchess County," she said, drooping a little inside the wired bodice of the strapless chiffon.

"I know, but Claude was explaining to me that up here it's very au naturel," Buddy said, relenting, dropping his hand on her shoulder. "I mean, Marie Antoinette and all that."

Corinne turned around for him to unzip her. It struck her

that she never looked naked to Buddy. She had put on a black garter belt and stockings to entice him, but as she slipped the chiffon dress down to her feet, she knew that Buddy was not watching. She felt mechanical and pure with him, a wooden dummy dressed up to please and, undressed, as neutral and sexless as a dummy between jobs in the shambles of a department store window. Buddy told her sometimes that she wore clothes well, and Corinne once asked him if he thought she unwore clothes well, which, as Buddy said with a smile, made no sort of sense at all.

She put on a skirt and silk blouse and went downstairs to fix herself a drink — a new habit — while Buddy shaved. She heard the water running upstairs; the old farmhouse was full of the noises of plumbing. Pipes ran down the corners of the rooms, and the heating system, recently added, grunted hot air through massive radiators. The house had a shabby charm which reminded Corinne of houses in the South before a bout of redecorating. Inside the closets, old wallpaper shone behind her city clothes.

She went to the radio and turned it on, searching for what Buddy called her cow music: the sweet, melted-together tunes of her girlhood, not quite recognizable without words. It was possible to find that music anywhere, she knew, and after fiddling with the knob for a while, she heard it — an overflow of honey, sticky and thick. She did not want Buddy to know what she was playing, and she turned it down, even though there was no way he could hear anything with the shower going full blast. He took long showers. She could count on ten more minutes alone. The radio was playing a mixture of "Dancing in the Dark" and "Blue Tango" — at least, one faded into the other so imperceptibly that they seemed mixed — and Corinne took to the center of the stripped pine floor and made a few turns. Outside the window, the shaggy New York State pastureland fell away to a strip of dark mountains. The river lay hidden somewhere between.

Buddy, coming down the steps in his seersucker, found his wife sitting on the couch, her feet together, her elbows at her sides.

"Have you been sitting there all this time?"

"I was thinking what we need to do to this room. We need to get rid of those great big radiators." They crouched in three corners, untamed metal beasts.

"That'd mean a whole new heating system. We can't afford it yet." He kissed her on her mouth. "Let's go sit on the porch, where we can see Claude."

"I don't want to look like we're hanging around, waiting for him," Corinne said, resisting Buddy's hand.

"Well, that's what we're doing, isn't it?" he asked, smiling. Then he noticed her wineglass, and the smile passed. "You don't want to get in the habit of drinking alone," he said, carrying her glass to the kitchen.

"Just a sip while I was waiting for you to dress. It takes you such a long time to dress," she couldn't resist adding.

"Wait till we get to the club," he said, tipping the wine out into the kitchen sink, then reaching up for the greasy frayed cord and jerking the flourescent light off. "Remember, Cory — we want to get on the waiting list. They've got three tennis courts and a golf course, and they're talking about putting in a pool."

"I never have been a member of a club."

"You'll enjoy it." He led her out to the screen porch and settled her in a creaking rattan rocker, after inspecting the crumpled cushion for dirt. "We need to join; it'll be fun, as well as helpful."

"I thought we came up here to be alone."

"We'll be alone enough," he said. "Saturday nights, we'll want somewhere to go."

She was silent, leaning her elbows on her knees, her chin in her hands. She wanted to ask the questions which circled, all the time, around the rim of her attention: why he did not turn to her, why it seemed as though they had been married ever since they were both children, why she could not remember when things happened. Her mother would tell her, if asked, that the flatness of her life was her own responsibility; no grown woman could expect her husband's undivided attention. And Cory lacked interests — she would have to agree with her mother, on that. Now and then Buddy suggested that she take another exercise class or a noncredit course in literature or a fast course in a language — anything, Corinne thought, to get her started. He had even mentioned volunteer work at a hospital. Corinne did not try to explain that she was waiting for the start, the lurch forward, which would come when she was pregnant. They had stopped talking about that a year before.

"There he is," Buddy said, jumping up, smiling with a kind of spasm which pinched up his face and made him look suddenly much older. He started off the porch, then turned back, almost with a creak, to hold the door open for Corinne. "Come on, Cory, we don't want to keep him waiting."

The big, dark green Mercedes sat uncertainly at the edge of the gravel road. Claude Hughes was peering out at the frayed white farmhouse and at the pair approaching him rapidly.

Buddy settled Corinne in the front seat and jumped in the back. He leaned over the seat to talk to Claude, who was backing the car out. In the dashboard light, Corinne could see his nimble patent-leather slippers, old enough to be cracked, with square black bows. Claude wore his slippers with everything, even corduroy slacks.

"I hope I was right. I told Cory not to dress," Buddy was saying. Corinne felt his warm breath by her ear and shuddered; it was as though he had touched her suddenly, intimately, through her skirt.

"This is such an informal little place, she could have come in an old cotton dress and nobody would even notice. I mean, these people have been coming up here for years," Claude said.

"That's what I thought." Buddy sounded relieved, but he did not lean back. "Nothing is worse than new people overdressing."

"I made some calls today, and they're going to put your names on the waiting list. Of course the election isn't until the fall. That gives you time to get to know some of the members. It'd be a good idea to give a party — nothing elaborate, cocktails outside, maybe some cheese — and then I can suggest sponsors."

"How many will we need?"

"The minimum is three, but to be absolutely certain, I think you should name at least five. I'll be able to point out some likely candidates tonight, so you can start to get to know them. No use, of course, to name people as sponsors unless you know them more than casually. A young couple from Riverdale — Merton, I think their name was; yes, Carey and something Merton — made that mistake, two years ago. People were affronted."

"That's the thing to avoid," Corinne said.

"What?" Claude looked at her, surprised.

"Affronting people."

"Of course!" The two men laughed. "Not much danger of that, though, sweetie," Claude said. "You two are just what we want."

Buddy sighed deeply and settled back into the seat.

The sun was setting as they drove along the two-lane tarmac road through the long valley that edged the Hudson. Corinne looked out, surprised to see dairy farms, apple farms. She had lived long enough in New York City to lose faith in the existence of the working country. Claude explained that most of the farms were fringe and would fail in the next few years; the economic health of the country would depend, increasingly, on the city people who came to renovate old houses along the river. It was wonderful to see the way they were influencing the yahoos. A farmers' market had been set up outside the city of Hudson, and the wives of two of the associates had seen to it that the oldest house in town was preserved and refurbished and opened to the public: Old Stone House, it was called; they would pass the historic marker.

"I want to plant a vegetable garden," Corinne said, abruptly. "Parsley, kale, okra, cabbage, broccoli, and sunflowers."

"Afraid it's a little late for that, this season," Claude said. "I can recommend an old guy for manure, though — takes it from his cow barn. You could get him to disc-harrow and manure, and then next spring you'd have a decent plot."

"But I want to can," Corinne said petulantly. "I want to freeze."

"Don't be silly, darling," Buddy said from the depths of the backseat.

Claude explained reasonably, "You're going to have to be patient. Or you could go to the farmers' market, get a big load of their produce, can and freeze it yourself."

"I have to grow it," Corinne said crossly. "That's why I came up here."

"News to me," Buddy said softly.

She turned, searching him out with her eyes. "I don't know why it's news to you. I told you I wanted a big freezer."

"Well, yes — sometime," he said, smiling.

"Right now. Tomorrow."

"Tomorrow's Sunday, darling."

"Well then what am I going to do up here all summer? When you go back to town? If I don't have a garden, or a freezer —"

"Good point," Claude said. "Never wise to be idle." Corinne looked at his white hands on the steering wheel.

"Why, honey, you can relax, for a change," Buddy said. "You won't have all those city responsibilities!"

She was quiet then, afraid of his sarcasm, afraid that Claude would understand.

Perhaps he did, for he dropped the subject and launched into a discussion of the membership of the club: which elderly ladies were the last of their family lines; which gentlemen cared about bridge and could be wooed that way; which members of the younger generation were likely to take an interest in keeping up the old family places. Corinne, listening, was impressed by his quick grasp of status; she could see all these strangers lined up as though for a parade, the elderly, distinguished grandmothers first, the callow teenagers at the rear. It seemed to her she was seeing her next twenty years, and she said after a while, "Claude, I wish I could meet them before you tell me which ones I ought to meet."

He laughed, reached over, and patted her hand, lying limp in her lap. "Don't worry, Corinne. You'll have a chance to form your own opinions."

"She always has plenty of those," Buddy said mildly, and again Corinne was silent. She was never sure when he might proceed, gently and calmly, to the attack; it usually began with a colorless remark of that kind.

She thought she loved him; there was no question in her mind that she had loved him once; and the fading color of their life together preoccupied her as though she had in fact drained the color out herself. She remembered meeting him on the *Queen Elizabeth* the last summer her parents had taken her abroad; she remembered the way he had cut across the dance floor to her; how he had taken her by the shoulders and turned her around to see the full moon through the lounge windows. He had seemed to know exactly how to treat her — handle her, she would have said, except that he had never really touched her: a kiss — good night — sweet and soft and quick, like the brush of a moth's wing; a hand at her back, or under her elbow, to guide her up a step.

Most boys had tumbled over her like puppies, grabbed at her, wanted to gum her mouth. Corinne had felt herself grow more delicate in the cool glow of his reverence.

He asked her to marry him the following May, after they had spent an agonizing winter apart, trying to arrange things to happen faster than Mrs. Mason wanted them to happen. Finally, in July, he came down with his ushers (all those smooth, handsome young men; they had names, but Corinne, and her mother, only thought of them as Buddy's ushers) and married her in a whirlwind. They had not been alone together since the previous Labor Day.

On their wedding night, he took her in his arms and told her that he loved her but that he was not up to sex. Towards morning, she woke to find that he was already in her. He came quickly, leaving her gasping, and rolled away. She lay a long time beside him, holding the spindles of the head-board with both hands.

One thing about southerners, she had thought, is that when they have made a choice, they hold on; like the snapping turtles in farm ponds who will hold a duck down by one leg till it drowns. She had held on to Buddy, and she meant to go on holding on to him, although sometimes she was so lonely with him she wanted to cry. It was not that they did not talk; they talked, almost continually, Buddy trying out his theories on her — theories about other people, their secrets, how they were motivated, small talk which made the world shrink. Now and then Corinne said she felt sure people behaved as they did for a multitude of reasons, only some of them petty, or evil — although the evil reasons might light up the field of speculation with a gaseous incandescent glow. Buddy, after agreeing with her, would go right on, analyzing, picking the grains of character apart. She wondered why they did not talk about themselves, about their loneliness; but then she knew she did not want to reduce it to that, the bare nub from which some kind of action would have to spring.

Claude turned the Mercedes into the club drive, and Corinne, looking out, was surprised to see that it was rutted and lined with tall weeds. Pinewoods, shabby with hanging limbs, fringed the drive, and ahead she could see the patched surface of an old golf course. Around the corner, three tennis courts lay behind sagging mesh fences.

Claude, as though understanding or anticipating her surprise, said, "The members don't care much about superficial charm." Ahead of them, Corinne saw the clubhouse, high on a hillock, white frame, with a broad front porch like a farmhouse's.

People were sitting on the porch. "Now don't be intimidated," Claude said, parking the Mercedes between a mud-smeared green pickup and a broken-looking yellow Jeep. He stepped out of the car and came around to open Corinne's door; she was waiting, gathering up her purse, putting her wits together. Buddy was already out and waiting, nearly dancing with excitement or nerves — Corinne was not sure which. His polka-dotted silk ascot reflected his blue eyes, his seersucker suit was fresh and crisp — she admired him for being so exactly suited to the occasion and felt, herself, rather shiftless and drab.

Claude herded them up the steps to the porch, where Corinne had the eerie sense of being introduced as if she was a relative to a group of strangers. Most of the members were elderly, and some of the men had difficulty standing up to shake her hand. The women, settled in the nests of their full skirts, did not get up at all. Their bright eyes, eager and curious, scanned the young couple, and Corinne found herself smoothing down her skirt, straightening her hair. At the same time, she felt entirely composed and comfortable. It was a familiar scene. As a child, she had been introduced into groups where bright eyes looked her over; her father would whisper to her under his breath, "Look well, look well, oh wolves" — for it was the pack judging, the gentle pack of gray-haired, toothless vixens: and she was prepared for their judgment, which was, in most cases, a foregone conclusion. "That Corinne Mason, you remember. Her eyes are exactly like her father's." Sometimes Cory had wondered what detail she would have needed to split their approval, to appear to them more strange than they could reasonably accept.

A dog, jingling metal tags from his collar, passed across the porch, and someone began to talk about hunting. Claude went to find drinks, which, Corinne realized, were laid out haphazardly in the kitchen. He returned to report that the ice was already gone, and a son was sent off to buy some more. There was speculation that the grocery store would be closed. Meanwhile the light was fading across the worn golf course, sinking down behind the farthest row of trees.

"In my day, the children came with their nurses," a tall, elderly woman told Corinne. She was looking with an absence of approval at a small knot of children playing football on the golf course. "They had their own supper, out there

under the pine trees, while we ate up here, and then someone would drive them home in time for baths and bed. Those
days are over," she said with asperity, "yet it seems to me
our young members might think occasionally of leaving the
children at home. I mean, there are sitters!" She looked at
Corinne out of bleached blue eyes. "Do you have any children, dear?"

"No," Corinne said, "not even a dog or a cat."

"That's very wise," the older woman said. "You're far too
young. As I said to Andrew, once we had children we might
as well forget about traveling, and I was a fanatic for traveling; we used to spend six months out of the year abroad."

"And did you?" Corinne asked, sitting down on the hard
bench by the edge of Mrs. Weatherford's violet wool skirt.

"Did I what?"

"Did you have children?"

"No," Mrs. Weatherford said and let the conversation
drop, turning to her neighbor, an old gentleman who was
propped up on a shooting stick. "Tell me, Madison, when
it rains do you sit on that or hold it over your head?"

He replied with a growl. Corinne, feeling excluded, got
up and went into the clubhouse with a vague notion of
seeing what it was like. After all, the dues were high. She
walked into the big room and stopped, struck by its resemblance to a hayloft: long, high, and light-filled, without a
scrap of furniture, although there was a handsome Turkish
rug on the floor. Dust hung in the last rays of light.

"I see you've found our pièce de résistance," a cracked
voice said behind her, and she turned to see another elderly
gentleman, tall as a crane, loping across the room. He was

eagerly smiling, and his breath smelled of copper; Corinne involuntarily drew back. "This room was used for square dances, in the old days," the crane said, looking wounded, drooping in front of her.

"I was thinking it might have been a hayloft."

"Well, you see it's not high enough off the ground." Reassured, he leaned towards her, his tall stick body bending from the hips, as though she was a coin he was examining, in a poor light. "Are you one of these New People? One of these ones that have come up from the city? Where do you live?"

"We've bought a little house in Claverack," she said circumspectly.

He flapped his elbows. "You'll be spending all your free time on improvements."

"I don't think we care that much about improvements."

"Much the wiser thing would be to invest in the old Fletcher place. You passed the gates on your way here. A pair of lions couchant in white limestone on top — you couldn't have missed them. Mimi Fletcher had to go to a nursing home last winter, and the house is sitting there disintegrating. A beautiful example of Dutch colonial, the double veranda, everything — simply waiting to be taken in hand." He looked at her brightly. "You really should involve yourself here."

"We're just trying it out," she said, although she knew Buddy would not be pleased with her answer.

"Well, that's not such a good idea, is it? I mean, with inflation you won't be able to buy next year what you can buy at a good price this year." He cranked his elbows up and down again, seemed to fill out, and spouted, "We need young blood up here!"

"Where are all your children?" she asked.

He seemed taken aback. "Do you mean personally?"

"Or impersonally," she said recklessly. Everything was upside down.

He regarded her sideways with a wise, bland smile. "Olivia and I were not blessed with children. My nephew and his wife however have been persuaded to come and spend the summer in our gatehouse. Two little girls, pretty things — you may have noticed them down there on the grass. We are hoping they will decide to settle here. The old Clifton place —" But he seemed to sense that he had gone far enough. Sadly, he concluded, "It is a precious life here, you must forgive us old vultures for trying to keep it going."

"Of course," she said warmly. He reminded her suddenly of her own father, and she was sorry to see him flap discreetly off.

A hedgehog-shaped man scurried past her with an enormous red casserole, which he dropped with a bang on the kitchen counter, exclaiming, "Hot! Hot!" and blowing on his small hands. Two women appeared with baskets of silver and napkins. Someone else went on all fours into a closet and resurrected a pile of dusty paper plates. Corinne found herself helping to lay all this out, neatly, on the counter. Then the cry went up — "Supper is on the table!" — which made Corinne smile since there was no table and only a kind of shorthand attempt at supper: the huge casserole of boiled chicken, limp inside its skin, and a paper platter of potato chips.

The flock hurried in from the porch, leaving behind the two Miss Esters, who cried out piteously; they were both confined to wheelchairs, and Corinne went to put food on plates, and carry them out. As she passed Buddy, he smiled at her and held up his fingers in a secret victory sign.

She wondered then at her own willingness to be useful, at her delight in it, even. Why was she being so charming? She could see her charm reflected in the smiles of the company, directed at her like warm rays. It's my training, she thought, unwilling to go any further than that, remembering that in the city there was no occasion for her to carry plates or cajole the appetites of bravely smiling elderly ladies.

I could be happy here, she thought, and was surprised.

She took a plate of food and sat down on the porch steps, where she was immediately joined by two elderly gentlemen, one red and spouting and eager, the other quiet and frayed, with a timid smile. It was hard work, entertaining them — they wanted to know more about her life than Corinne was ready to reveal — and the boiled chicken grew cold on her plate. Finally the frayed one cried, "We must let the poor girl eat!" Then they sat watching her chew. "Such extraordinary hair," the red one remarked, and very carefully touched the curl that lay on Corinne's shoulder. Buddy came over to take her plate, and reached down, with one hand, to help her up. She put her hand into his and was struck by how cold and seamy his skin felt; not cold, she corrected herself, but chilly, soft, and creased, like the underbody of a snake. Pleased to death with her, he took her inside to introduce her to Mrs. Vandermeer, who had cooked the chicken. Corinne found herself ablaze with compliments. Suddenly she was tired. Buddy had his smooth hand under her elbow, and she felt propped, passed along. "Now we will go and help ourselves to some of those beautiful strawberries," Buddy said. "Young Elkhorn — he's the tall blond with the wire-rimmed glasses — grew them on his farm. He's invited us to come over tomorrow for a strawberry tea." He was propelling her towards the kitchen, his hand soft yet irresistible under her elbow. They were fielding smiles, on each side, as the crowd fell away from them.

"I don't want any strawberries, thank you," Corinne said. "I think I'll take a little walk outside, get some air." She separated her elbow from Buddy's palm and turned on her heel, still nodding and smiling at the flock, which parted again to let her walk to the door. Buddy went on towards the kitchen and the big bowl of strawberries, and she heard him saying to someone, "What a feast! I mean, really —" She lost the rest as she stepped off the porch.

It was nearly dark. She could see the outlines of the tennis courts, and the dark pines along the road. She wanted to be hidden for a moment from the smiling, congratulatory eyes. She ran down the hill and stopped at the bottom, feeling the coolness. During the day, the heat had made her think of a southern summer, but now she smelled the damp of swamps and skunk cabbage, the unformed freshness of the spring.

She went along towards the pines. Then she heard children's voices and stopped, uneasy. Going closer, she saw a group seated around a small fire, roasting marshmallows on sticks. The firelight lit up their faces, shone on their long bare legs, and she wondered suddenly what she had been doing before, up there on the porch. Children always drew her. She walked towards them, and they turned as her foot broke a stick. "Who's there?" a man's voice cried, and she saw a tall figure stand up from its crouch by the fire. "Friend or foe?"

"Friend!"

"Come closer, then!"

The children all turned around as she stepped into the circle of the firelight, and Corinne imagined the figure she made against the background of dark trees.

The tall man came closer, bending to peer into her face. "Ah, you're the new blood," he said. "Do you want a marshmallow?" And he waved a stick at her.

"I certainly do!"

He took the half-melted marshmallow off his stick and dropped it into her palm. "Sit down here and roast some for yourself," he said. "Or are you afraid of dirtying your pretty dress?"

She sat on the ground, by the fire.

The children flocked around her, the younger ones coming close enough to touch — Corinne reached out, brushed her fingers against a fringe of sun-blond hair, a small ear — the older ones lurking in the shadows. The light from the fire, illuminating their faces, changed them into triangles or squares of white, without color or features, pieces of cut paper against the dark pine trees. Some were roasting marshmallows conscientiously; others had already tired of the treat and were grappling on the ground. Corinne realized suddenly that she had never known children except as a bunch. "Who are all these?" she asked the young man.

He ran off a litany of names. She recognized some of the surnames she had heard on the porch. The first names had the androgynous touch of class, or they were last names, preserved in amber: Lloyd, Dean, Brooke, Caufield. She wondered if these children, sexless already in their jeans and grimy shirts, grew up freer because their names were shared, generation after generation. They all knew one another well, the young man explained, having spent their summers together since they were small.

"And what is your name?" she asked, spreading the old southern coyness like a coating of caramel over her ordinary voice.

"I don't have any name, I don't need one," he said quickly. "I belong to Mrs. Madison Dixon."

"The old lady up on the porch — ?"

"I wouldn't call her old!"

"I mean, middle-aged, so handsome, that lovely gray hair . . . " She could not carry it on any longer. "Are you her son?" she asked cautiously, after a while.

He was poking up the embers with a stick. "Well, in a manner of speaking."

"I don't understand riddles."

"I do some of the things for her a son might do."

"He drives," one of the older boys explained. "Auntie Maudie can't drive because of her eyes. She can't see anything in the dark. She can see fine in the light," he added.

"I help her with her gardening — she's a fierce gardener, and it's more fun for her if she has someone to instruct. I've learned all the names of the flowers —"

"Did you know wild carrot is the same as Queen Anne's

lace?" a pretty dark-haired girl asked, edging in on the conversation, as though to ward off a revelation. Corinne began to understand that the older children knew about the young man's arrangements.

"What else do you do for her?" she asked, laying the candy aside.

"I fuck her," he said calmly. "She likes that, too."

Some of the younger children shrieked and rolled away on the grass. The older ones went on listening attentively.

"Oh," Corinne said. She poked her stick in farther among the coals, and her marshmallow toppled off and went up in a thin, separate plume of black smoke. "I thought I met a Mr. Dixon —"

"Want another?" He was at her elbow with the cellophane bag. "Don't pretend to be shocked," he said.

Taking out a marshmallow, she glanced at him. He had pearly skin, not tanned, but faintly rosy, as though he had spent all month outside under the pierced protection of a straw hat or an old-fashioned lace parasol. His ears were small; they lay close to his head, under the edge of his neatly trimmed blond hair. His cheeks were smooth; she wondered if he shaved, and ran from that into a question about his age. He seemed as skinny as a boy, yet she could not quite credit his frankness, if he was so young. Perhaps he was joking with her. Again she felt at sea. She longed to ask more questions but was prevented by the presence of the children.

"Auntie Maudie's husband had a stroke. He can't hardly walk," a girl with dark braids explained. "So she got Peter." She twirled the end of one braid, smiling.

115

"Peter!" Corinne smiled at him. "I have half your name."

"Peter Martin, the same as the ballet dancer," an older girl explained politely.

"That's Martins," Peter said. "Your Auntie Maudie would never put up with anything from the ballet."

"Why not?" a boy wanted to know.

Corinne asked, at the same time, "Is she all their aunt?" She knew the construction was wrong.

"Everybody's, except for Sheila," a blond boy explained. "Sheila isn't related to anybody." And he cuffed a girl who was sitting with her knees drawn up, a little to the side. She tumbled over obediently and whimpered.

Peter set on the boy, throwing him down on his back and holding him there with one hand. "I'll teach you to torment ladies!"

"I am too related," Sheila whined, still prone. "I'm related to Mrs. Milton!"

"She's somebody's cousin," another child chimed in. "I mean, fourth or fifth cousin. That doesn't count."

Peter let the boy up. He came rushing at him, and Peter grabbed him in his arms and upended him again. The child stayed on his back this time, staring up at the pine branches overhead.

"I also see to the children," Peter told Corrine. "I'm a jack-of-all-trades."

"He teaches us tennis," the solemn boy who had spoken first explained, and Corinne understood that he was trying to make the situation appear ordinary. "We all take lessons every day."

"He lives with Auntie Maudie, in her guest room with the four-poster bed," the girl with braids explained.

"Well, sometimes," Peter said shyly.

Corinne was beginning to understand the way he joked. He had a way of shooting his words at her as though they were partners; partly the result, she guessed, of having been exclusively with the children all evening, so that any adult seemed a confederate. "Want to know something?" he asked, crawling near her, and Corinne stared again at his flushed, smooth skin and wondered how he would look in electric light. "I have never in my life been up on that porch."

"Auntie Maudie said it would bore him to death," the girl named Brooke explained, and the older children, as though to shield Peter, began to recite a litany of the porch: how dreary it was, how quiet one had to be, how few soft drinks were available, and how likely the food was to run out before the children, always the last in line, were allowed to get something to eat. "It's nice down here, though," the worried boy named Shelton announced, looking at Corinne for confirmation.

"I wasn't too crazy about the porch,' she said.

Then Peter announced that they were going to play a game — all of the marshmallows had been eaten, and the younger children, bored by the talk, were beginning to fight. He explained to Corinne that the game was indigenous to Wildwood. One child would be selected secretly by Peter to be the murderer, and the others were all his potential victims. After the murder, they would have a trial, and the winner would be the one who identified the assassin. By this time, the children were hopping with eagerness, their bare legs flashing as they darted around the dying fire. Peter went from one to the other, cupping his hands over their ears and whispering. Some of the older girls shuddered and skipped, and Corinne imagined the way his warm breath made their ears tingle. He passed her by, indicating with a raising of his eyebrows that she was not expected to play the game.

"But I want to!" she cried.

Peter stopped, turned back; she noticed his long back, his small buttocks, the narrowness of his thighs. "You'll ruin your dress, going through the brambles."

"That doesn't matter," she said stoutly.

"OK." He bent over her, cupping his hands around her right ear. "I'd like to fuck you," he whispered.

She turned her head away. In spite of herself, a heavy blush crept over her face.

Before she had decided on a reaction, Peter was leading the children into the woods.

Corinne was alone. The fire was dying; the shadows of the trees gathered around her. In the distance, she could see the light of the clubhouse, shining between the trunks of the pines. She stood up slowly, brushing off her skirt. It occurred to her that she could simply turn and walk back to the clubhouse, climb up on the porch, and pick up a conversation. There was no reason in the world not to go back. Buddy would probably be looking for her. There were a good many people she had not yet spoken to, and some of them were sure to be interesting or influential or both. She felt stale at that thought, as though she was thumbing through a handful of wrinkled greasy bills. Interesting or influential or both.

She took a few steps, undecided. It was turning cold, and she grasped her elbows in her hands. Peter's breath in her ear had been as warm as she had imagined it when she had watched him whispering to the little girls, as warm and as anonymous. Even his words had been anonymous, and the flash of his eyes, afterwards, had been like the flash of head-lights. She felt his chill, his distance, his power. He had used a word she used only when she was lying on her stomach, in bed, creeping one hand, a slow crab, between her thighs. Fuck was the power she had never felt, the name-less faceless power of the intruder. She wondered what she thought now about gentleness, the quality she had prized all her life. Such a gentle man. Such a gentleman. Peter's breath had no quality of gentleness in it.

Away in the trees, she heard a child shriek. Suddenly she was terrified that the game was already over. She winced and gasped and drew herself together. As she took the first step into the woods, she understood that she would never be able to blame anyone for the consequences. Alone. I am alone, she thought.

Driving home to Claverack, Corinne sat in the front seat next to Buddy while Claude, too drunk to drive, lounged in the back. It was late. Green light from the dashboard fell on the stained panels of Corinne's skirt. Claude sang a song about monkeys and mongrels and laughed loud and long into the silence. "You saw them, you saw them," he kept repeating gleefully. "You saw them in all their glory."

"I liked them," Buddy said. He was clutching the steering wheel and leaning forward to peer into the darkness. "I think we will make some very congenial friends at the club. Don't you think so, Cory?" He did not look at her, but his right ear seemed to lean, hopefully, in her direction.

"Yes, I think we will," she said.

"Cory was the belle of the ball," Claude cried. "The invisible belle of the ball!"

"I told you, I was down with the children."

"You two planning on any?"

"In due course," Buddy said.

"How long you been married, anyway?"

"Seven years," Corinne said smoothly, to spare Buddy.

"Isn't that due course?"

"Cory has a little problem," Buddy said. "We're going to get that cleared up, first."

"She doesn't look like she has a problem in the world. Leaves in her hair, is all!" Claude leaned forward carefully and picked a pine needle out of the back of Cory's hair.

Corrine looked at her husband. She had heard him give many explanations, when friends or family were unkind enough to force the issue, but she had never before heard him refer to her problem. She wondered what image, if any, formed in his mind when he said those words. She thought of her vulva, which she had seen once in a hand mirror, pink and curled and layered, mysterious, complex; did he imagine a gate there, an unmanageable lock? She wanted to ask him what he imagined, and it did not seem strange that for the first time she could listen to him without irritation as though he was describing, when he described her, the ridges and declivities in his own mind. Oh Buddy, honey, what do you see? She regretted that Claude, stretching in the backseat, was there to prevent the question. The answer might have made Buddy appear, for the first time, clear, separate, and whole.

At their door, Claude slid out. He opened Corinne's door

and kissed her cheek as she climbed out. "Good night, Belle!"

"Good night, Claude. Thank you for introducing us."

Buddy, however, turned sharply aside.

"He's tired," Corinne explained. "We almost never stay up this late."

"Call me tomorrow," Claude said. "I want to know what he thought. Really, I mean, it's a bunch of old gasbags, but I thought you'd both find it amusing." He hunched himself and climbed into the driver's seat as though he was climbing into a cave.

"I think you hurt Claude's feelings," Corinne said, following Buddy into the kitchen and turning on the blue fluorescent light.

"Turn off that light," he said. "I'm going to bed. It's nearly three o'clock in the morning."

In bed, he snatched her, flipped her, and inserted his penis. He was already hard. Corinne took the corner of the pillow in her mouth.

CHAPTER EIGHT

*T*HE BROWN HOTEL on a rainy Tuesday at noon smelled of wet raincoats and wool sweaters damp around the neck. The lobby was full of people who swirled in and out of the revolving doors, or waited by the glossy elevators whose brass was shined hourly by a negro in a blue-and-crimson uniform with gold buttons and epaulets. His other function was to empty the brass cuspidors and refill them with snowy sand; before they were emptied, the sand was starred with cigar butts and crumpled cigarette ends, some stained with a lipstick called Cherry Blossom — a brilliant magenta which was the big seller at Stewarts, down the block.

Behind the desk, the cloakroom was full of ladies' coats, plastic slickers, sleek, damp brown-and-white boxes and bulky shopping bags. A year before, Stewarts had changed to green and white to promote a campaign called Springtime in Kentucky; there had been such an outcry at the change, which effaced a treasured connection with the brown-and-white boxes brought back, occasionally, from a big department store in New York, that the green and white had disappeared overnight.

The ladies who met their husbands for lunch on that rainy Tuesday wore spike heels in dark colors, nylons with seams, and hats with a smidgen (as the advertisements put it) of veil. The veils had an odd effect on the noses of some of the older ladies; the cells of the net seemed to magnify the pores of the skin. However, none of the husbands would have dreamed of remarking on the unflattering effect; it was important for wives of whatever age to maintain a fashionable appearance so that the dim fear, which surfaced at times in the drunken behavior of certain members of the community, the dim fear, with its sharply cutting edge, that this was just a little town, a little town lost at the edge of a big muddy river, might sink in a sea of white tissue paper, capsized shoe boxes, and fluttering, pale pink bills.

Hammond Mason, waiting for his sister in the lobby, spoke to one acquaintance after another as they passed him on their way to The River Room. Some of the younger men who were escorting dates took the stairs up to the restaurant, but the settled couples aimed for the elevators.

After they spoke to Hammond — everyone knew who he was waiting for, and inquired after the health of his sister, Polly — they spoke to Curtis, the negro in the blue-and-crimson uniform. At lunchtime it was difficult for Curtis to attend to his work because there were so many white people to speak to, to recognize by name, with a tiny bow and scrape, a miniature version of the exaggerated obeisances of his father, the spoons player with the Old Jug Band. "How's

Omar?" the older men asked Curtis; they remembered Omar prancing across the dance floor, flicking his spoons, at the debutante parties of the previous generation. "Coming along," Curtis would tell them. Omar lived with Curtis, and his querulous old age was a burden to the younger man. The other members of the Jug Band had died: Carlton, who had played the comb; Dixie, who had sawed the fiddle; and big Mac, the leader, who had exhaled snorts into the brown whiskey jug. Omar, bitterly alone, made his son's life a hell, but when Curtis greeted the white people in the lobby of the hotel, he never thought of that. He thought of their smiles as they came towards him through the crowd.

It was not like Polly to keep anyone waiting, and Hammond, feeling uneasy, went to telephone her apartment. Polly had moved into town when her husband died, abandoning the old house on Locust Road, where she and Hammond had grown up.

The desk clerk at The 700 answered that Mrs. Rose had pased through the lobby a half hour before. Hammond guessed that Polly had left in time to walk to the Brown and had then been sidetracked by a friend or a display in a shop window.

He wandered around the crowded lobby, his hands in his pockets, speaking to old friends. At one point, he stopped to study the large river bass, mounted on a board, which had been caught in the lobby by a bellboy during the '37 flood. Hammond remembered the excitement of the flood. He had manned a rowboat and single-handedly evacuated a half dozen negro families from the west end. He remembered the silence of the flooded streets, the peaks of the shotgun houses coming out of the water, and the faces of the people, sitting on their roofs, watching for him to come and save them.

It did not seem unreasonable to wish that life had held a few more such moments. During the war, Hammond had served as corporal at Fort Knox until an old back injury put him out of commission; in the twenty-five years since, he had become aware of steadily increasing restlessness. Remembering his own father's troubled times, he took what precautions he could: cut down on his drinking, controlled his flirtations, spent more time at home. It helped. The itch faded, or changed to an ache. Looking at the stuffed bass, Hammond realized that the ache would be with him for the rest of his life.

"I'm *so* sorry," Polly said, behind him, and Hammond turned, taking his hands out of his pockets to grasp his sister's shoulders. Polly put her face down — she was a tall woman — so that Hammond could kiss her, quickly, on the cheek. Her skin smelled, dependably, of Hines Honey-and-Almond cream — one of the few pleasures of Hammond's sensual life. Polly was a remarkably clean woman. Her eyes, behind blue-rimmed glasses, were clear, the whites as pearly as a girl's, and her creased, soft skin looked scrubbed. Hammond remembered her bathroom at The 700. ("No window," she had remarked, sadly, remembering the window looking into the heart of a big magnolia in the house on Locust.) On the imitation-marble sink, a row of scrubbing devices had been laid out on a clean white hand towel: pumice, nail brush, complexion brush, and an odd orange rubber thing for the scalp.

Polly made up in cleanliness, Hammond thought, for what she lacked in attractiveness. She was too tall, too massive and large-featured to be considered pretty, although everyone agreed that she was handsome, an ambiguous compliment for a single woman in a town known for its tiny, delicate ladies. At one point, Hammond had hoped that Polly might remarry — she was only fifty-five; but the first time he had seen her, a widow out of mourning at an evening party, he had noticed the width of her shoulders in her strapless, pale blue dress and realized that no one in town was likely to take their owner on.

"Don't worry about keeping me waiting. I've reserved a table, and you know Marcus will save it for us." He helped her out of her coat and smelled her perfume — Claire de Lune — rising from the collar. He carried the coat to the cloakroom, took his ticket from Addie (a chambermaid recently promoted), and went back to find Polly engulfed in a crowd of well-wishers. Since she had moved to The 700, she was not seen as frequently as when she had been ensconced, entertaining regularly, on Locust Road, so her appearances were greeted with a flurry of questions. "I would love to have you all over before the symphony," Hammond heard her explain, "but you know I only have that little tiny dining nook, and I simply have to resign myself to no more than three for a meal."

He separated her expertly from her questioners and propelled her into the elevator. "What a mercy," she said to him softly. "You know my new arrangement spares me *so much*." Hammond did not need an interpretation. He knew his sister had developed a passion for eating hamburgers and potato chips in front of the television set, an unthinkable indulgence in the high Victorian dining room on Locust Road.

"Middle age has *some* compensations," he said mildly.

Polly looked at him speculatively. There were five other people in the elevator, all of them first-name friends, so of course it was impossible to continue; Hammond saw his sister bite down on her words. He could count, always, on her discretion, which provided him with a pleasure almost equal to the pleasure he took in her cleanliness. They were, as everyone in town remarked, close.

Curtis drew back the gilded gate as the elevator stopped, and its occupants trooped out and hesitated at the door of The River Room. On Tuesday, the favorite lunch day, every table was taken, and a roar of conversation greeted the newcomers. Waiters in blue-and-crimson uniforms moved between the white-linen-covered tables, carrying big oval tin trays high over their heads. The headwaiter, a mulatto named Marcus Williams, stood surveying the scene with a critical eye. Marcus had been known to ask drunken white gentlemen to leave; one of the great delicacies of the town, a hot, deep red steak sauce, was named after the formidable headwaiter whose bite, it was said, was nearly as sharp.

"Morning, Mr. Mason," Marcus said, without looking at Hammond. "I saved you the table in the corner." It was his usual place, apart from the rest.

"That's good of you, Marcus. I'm sorry we're late. My sister was slightly delayed."

Used to irrelevant apologies and long-winded excuses, Marcus continued to gaze away over the top of the crowd.

After a suitable interval, he beckoned to a young waiter and told him to show Mr. Mason and Mrs. Rose to their table. As he passed, Hammond slid a folded bill into Marcus's limp, half-open hand.

Hammond pulled out a chair for his sister, then sat down across from her with his back to the room. He preferred not to spend his lunch nodding and waving at acquaintances; Polly, more oblivious, would forget about them in five minutes. Meantime she bowed and smiled, and Hammond ordered two glasses of dry sherry. "There's a chill in the air," he remarked, to explain his choice, "even though it's summer."

"My feet are wet; I shouldn't have walked over, but I get to feeling pent up in The 700," Polly said, spreading out the big menu. "What do you think?"

"You always take the Brown Sandwich," Hammond said.

"That's so heavy." Polly sighed. "Did you notice I've put on weight?" She plucked at the waistband of her navy blue skirt.

"You know you really don't need to worry about an extra pound or two," Hammond said, looking at the menu.

"I think Marcus would do better to forgo the seafood. Everybody knows we're too far inland to get anything fresh."

"Well, at least they don't offer dried cod. You remember when we used to have dried cod in cream sauce every Friday?"

"For that housemaid of Mother's who was Irish. She left finally in a flood of tears because she couldn't stand being in the middle of black people."

They laughed softly. The old stories bound them together.

"We were lucky, growing up. We knew what was expected of us, we knew what we could count on," Hammond went on, signaling to the waiter to take their order. "I sometimes think it's not so easy for Corinne and Apple."

"You and Adeline have always made their situation perfectly clear,' Polly said, taking a sip of water. The ice cubes clinked against her large teeth.

"Well, we tried. But it hasn't always worked. You know how Adeline felt about Cory getting married so young. She talked and talked to her, she gave her the best reasons, and Cory listened perfectly calmly and then went right out and did as she pleased."

"Well, that's water over the dam. Cory seems to be doing well."

"From all we hear, which isn't much. She hasn't been down since last Thanksgiving, and then we didn't really talk." Hammond felt that it was ignoble to complain, but he missed his elder daughter. The sympathy between them, the old closeness, was stretched as thin as a thread since she had moved to New York; her weekly letters were mere accounts, and none of them liked to talk on the telephone. "I guess no news is good news," Hammond said, sighing heavily, and wished he had not brought up the subject; his sadness about Cory could not really be explained, and he was afraid it might be interpreted as the grasping possessivenes of an overly attached father. "Probably the best thing in the world for her to get out of here early," he muttered.

"You *are* in a dreary mood. Well, at least you don't have anything to reproach yourself with on Apple's account."

"Adeline's not too pleased."

"What does Adeline have against Billy Long?"

"She says he's common. Common as dirt, to use her exact words."

The brother and sister were silent. Adeline's fine social sense had often come between them; they did not need words to communicate the mixture of awe and distaste it provoked. They remembered a simpler time before Hammond's marriage, when anyone equipped with charm was considered perfectly all right, when the town had been smaller and it had not been necessary to erect barriers against strangers.

"And it's true," Hammond said, coming quickly to his wife's defense. His silence had seemed a veiled attack. "He is a perfecctly ordinary young man. You know he works for me. I've had opportunities to observe him. Billy Long keeps to the middle of everything. Just the right degree of ambition. Just the right degree of independence. He won't go far, but he'll go the right amount to be well thought of yet not envied. He has it all figured out."

"Well, there are worse things," Polly said.

"He's not a cad and he's not a bounder, to use some more of dear Adeline's favorite words. But he is — well, perfectly ordinary."

"That's not the same thing as common as dirt. You think he has designs on Apple? She's so young!"

"No, it's not the same thing," Hammond said.

Then he was silent.

After a while, Polly asked, "Do you think he —"

"Yes," Hammond said, with a ripple of impatience in his

voice. It was the most he allowed himself. "Yes," he forced himself to repeat. "Billy Long has designs on my younger daughter, Apple."

"Why are you making it an announcement?" Polly asked, glancing around uneasily. Several women at the next table had looked up, their forks suspended.

"Was I speaking loudly?"

The women looked down at their plates again.

"Not the volume so much as the tone!" Polly said.

"I'm sorry." They waited while Benny, the waiter, slid their orders in front of them. Then Polly said, "Hammond, honey, give Apple some advice."

He shook his head. "Once I see something like that starting to happen, I know there's nothing in the world I can do to stop it, and so I just want to get it over with as quickly as possible. I wish they were getting married tomorrow, to tell you the truth," he said, with a rush of feeling which he could only permit himself with Polly, who would, of course, know that he was exaggerating. "What is the use of floundering around, preoccupied with a question that was already answered months ago? When he gave her that first riding lesson, I saw it was settled. Apple has always had a naive respect for authority."

"That's why the two of you get on so well," Polly said, tilting her smile towards her brother, who finally noticed it and responded with a slight pained grin.

"Oh, I know I'm ridiculous about my daughters," he said, picking at his sandwich, which looked too brown and shiny under its layer of sauce.

"You love them," Polly said simply. "I always thought if

131

Pickle and I had been blessed, I would have made an absolute fool of myself over our issue." She said our issue ironically, to draw the string.

"Pickle used to tell me he was a proven stud, when he'd had a few drinks," Hammond said.

"That poor Missy Pike down in Bowling Green with those two lummoxes of boys. I told Pickle they may have proved something about him but it wasn't anything to brag about," Polly replied gallantly, but she was hurt; Hammond saw her take a long sip of iced water.

He reached over and patted her large, freckled hand. "I'm sorry, honey. I get mean as a hornet when I think about losing Apple."

"Gaining a son, not losing —"

"Very nice, but Billy Long will never be a son to me. Not in any sense."

"Well, you are too choosy."

"It's one of the saddest things I can think of that you and Pickle didn't have children," he said, to change the subject.

Polly, chewing, looked at him. He did not press the question, but she felt his curiosity like an elbow in her side. They had never really gone into the details, and now, plagued as he was with worries about Apple and Cory, only the details of Polly's infertility could distract him.

"What really was the problem?" he asked.

"I know you've always wondered." Polly laid down her fork and wiped her mouth with the white damask napkin. The stain of lipstick she left on the napkin was vivid, and she considered it for a moment, preparing herself. "There isn't a reason in the world not to talk about it now. Pickle's been in Cave Hill Cemetary five years, and I never even hear his name mentioned anymore. When I think how he used to be in the paper every week or so, winning the Country Club golf tournament, catching that enormous catfish in the Ohio when everybody claimed sewage had killed off all forms of life —"

"Nothing ever kills the catfish."

"And now even the people who used to see him every day at the office don't mention him to me. It's as though he never lived." She laid the napkin across her lap and took another sip of water. "It's a relief to talk about him, to tell you the truth, Hammy." He was startled to hear her use the old nickname which they had agreed years before to abandon; startled but not displeased, for it indicated a new intimacy between them. "The truth is, Pickle never could win enough trophies or get talked about enough. He was always on the go, and a lot of it wasn't purely business. One time after we'd been married a year and a half he went down to New Orleans on some cockamamy business and came back with a bad case of you-know-what." She gazed at him under level brows. "That was when old Dr. Jeffers was still prescribing mercury, and it left him impotent. That's the whole story," she said, as though she saw the disappointment Hammond was trying to hide.

"All these years wondering, and it was nothing but a good case of the clap!" he cried, aggrieved.

"Hush." The ladies at the next table, having heard too much already, turned away in a discreet murmur of conversation. "It was syphilis. Nowadays, of course, he'd be given a shot of penicillin and that would be the end of that.

When I was mad at him, I used to say he lost our children in a Louisiana cathouse."

Hammond stared at his sister. He saw a slow, painful blush rise up out of the frilled collar of her white blouse, travel around her jaws, and end in the lobes of her ears. She stared down at her plate, poking at the edge of the sandwich with her fork. "My appetite's gone," she said. "Why did we have to begin on all that?"

"I'm sorry, honey." He reached over and clasped her hand.

"I guess the truth is I've always wanted to tell you. Not to get the poison out, but because I wanted you to appreciate your girls, to appreciate the precious gift —" She looked up, her eyes glazed with tears, and pressed the edge of her napkin to her lips. "Not that you ever seemed to take them for granted, but I sometimes thought Adeline was too hard on them, and I wished I could have made her see how precious —"

"I know what you mean," Hammond said. "Poor Adeline. They never can seem to measure up to what she expects. I don't know what it is she expects, and sometimes I think she doesn't either, but whatever it is, neither Apple nor Cory has much chance of measuring up to it."

"What is it?" Polly asked, pushing her plate away. "No, Hammy, I really want to know," for he had flicked his head, nervously, irritably. "I've told you the darkest secret I've ever had" — she laughed — "and here you don't want to tell me one thing about Adeline. No, I want to know! What is it she expects from those girls?"

"Dessert, Colonel?" The waiter thrust two large menus under their noses.

"Nothing but coffee," Hammond said, waving the menus away. "All right," he went on. "I'll tell you what it is Adeline expects — fair's fair, after all!" The expression reminded them both of the rainy afternoons they had spent playing in the attic of the old house on Locust Road.

"Fair's fair!" Polly repeated softly. They did not need to elaborate on the shared memory. It was one of many: when Hammond had tried to tell her the facts of life, for instance, and Polly, wincing, had stuffed her fingers in her ears.

"She expects them to be perfect," Hammond said, "in some awful way, the way she is perfect. I mean perfect-looking, to begin with — hair done every Tuesday at Mr. James's, nails manicured, beautiful clothes ordered from the New York catalogs. Cory always refused to have anything to do with that. You remember how sloppy she looked when she was going to school —"

"She managed to make that navy blue uniform look draggle-tailed. I never knew how."

"And then fat, for a while. Adeline never could forgive Cory for liking chocolate sundaes and getting fat when she was fourteen. I tried to explain to her that it was hormones, something like that (old Dr. Baker even backed me up, would you believe it, gave Adeline a lecture about adolescence), but none of it had a bit of effect on Adeline. She said Cory was self-indulgent. Oh, she said it a lot. Cory used to just look at her. If looks could kill, as they say. Then of course she'd go out and eat more and what would probably have worn off in a year lasted three. That took her into her debut, and Adeline had to drag her to New York and take her to the stubby department, or whatever it's called, to buy her all those long dresses."

"I remember Adeline saying Cory never wore an evening dress twice. I told her it was a terrible waste."

"Yes, but they were all size sixteens. I remember Adeline showing me the label. Just showing me the label — nothing needed to be said. Cory didn't thin down till she met Buddy, and then Adeline knew that they were sleeping together — jumped up in the middle of the night after we'd been talking to Cory on the telephone and said, 'I know, just know, they're sleeping together,' which was another form of self-indulgence, to Adeline. A worse form. 'You are forfeiting all possibility of future hapiness,' Adeline told her."

Polly sighed. You remember that springer spaniel I had — Daisy? Years ago?"

"Yes," Hammond said, still pursuing his own thoughts.

"Well, the first time she went into heat, she ran off, and I searched the neighborhood for her. Finally saw her running through the weeds with two ugly-looking black-and-tan dogs. I saw her running, and I saw the grin on her face, and I caught her and whopped her with my belt. My heart was beating — I don't think I'll ever forget that. I put her in the kennel every time she was in heat, after that."

"Daughters are not the same things as bitches," Hammond said.

"Well, of course not, dear — I'm not a fool! I was talking about my personal reaction to that sort of thing." Polly leaned back so that the waiter could fill her cup with coffee. Then she poured a little milk out of the chrome pitcher, and Hammond noticed that her hand was trembling.

"I guess we could do without raking up the past," he said, feeling sorry for her, as he felt when he called for her at The 700 and watched her come rustling out of her bed-room, all smiles, handing him her fur jacket. "I've upset you now, you won't be able to enjoy your shopping."

Polly said, "I was just going to look for stockings."

"Now I feel bad."

"Well, don't. We're both at the age where we have to begin to think about what we've lost. Anyway, we got on this subject talking about Adeline, and I'm no nearer now than I was then to understanding what it is she expects." She flung the gauntlet down and continued, into his silence, "All the years I've known Adeline, and she's as obscure to me as she was that first time we had lunch, right in this room! I watched her take off her gloves and put them in her glass (you remember, that was the old sign that a lady didn't want a drink), and I thought then, I'll never understand her. Pretty as a picture and just as pleasant but with some-thing — everything — hidden away. Now you must tell me what I've missed."

"That's more than I bargained for. I was only trying to tell you what she expected from the girls."

"Well, I guess I'll have to settle for that," she said.

"I've told you what she feels about appearances — ap-pearances! That's the wrong word! Appearances mean more than anything else to Adeline — maybe because she really believes you can lie with words but you can't lie with the way you look: taste is the touchstone, you know? So she had her battles with the girls on that front. But then, beyond that, she wanted them both to have more education. She was sick when Cory got married so young. She wanted Apple to try to get into some college in the East even though

Apple's grades wouldn't qualify her for the state university. That's been a major disappointment for Adeline. You know she was bright, did so well in school, went ahead and graduated from Sweet Briar. She feels an education makes up for a lot of the inevitable disappointments in life. You know how she reads, how she writes letters. Apple never reads, and Cory doesn't appear to know how to write more than a summary."

Polly sipped her coffee. "You're not telling me a thing I didn't already know," she said after a while. "Now why is that?"

"Because it's all I know myself," he said.

People were standing up, shoving in their chairs, dropping their napkins over the wreckage of their lunches. Hammond felt an urge to leave. After all, he had pushed the limits of their conversation further than he had intended, and still Polly gazed at him in that bright, beady way, like a bird which sees a seed lying just out of reach; he could imagine the quick dart of her long neck, the snap of her lips on the tidbit. He had no tidbits for her. He stood up and pulled her chair out, feeling her surprising weight. "I have to get back to work."

She twisted around, looking at him. "Well, of course, if it's time to go . . ." She stood up, waiting while he paid the bill.

"Nice to see you again, Mr. Mason," Marcus said without looking at them as they passed. Hammond waved Polly into the elevator, and they rode down in silence.

As he was helping her into her coat, Polly said in a low, troubled voice, "I hope I haven't offended you, Hammond."

He squeezed her shoulder, kissed her cheek. "Of course you haven't offended me. You couldn't offend me if you tried."

"Well, you seemed so —"

"It's all the things I don't understand, myself. They kind of rose up before me. Here I've been living with Ady for thirty years, and I can't even explain what she expects of our daughters." He shook his head, standing stoop-shouldered, blocking the path to the revolving door. Several friends passed by without speaking. "It makes me feel ridiculous," Hammond said.

Polly steered him towards the door. There was a press of people behind them. She stepped into a compartment, and Hammond pushed himself into the one behind her. The door turned quickly, yet in that instant Hammond saw, as though through a magnifying glass, the gray hairs which lay scattered untidily on her neck. Polly was aging. In another year or two she would begin to look actively old. He shuddered as he stepped out onto the damp sidewalk.

They both looked down Broadway. There was a steady procession of cars passing along the wet pavement; the pale blue streetlamps had been turned on early, and the store windows shone with yellow light. It was a pleasant, bustling scene.

"I'll see you next Tuesday?" Hammond asked.

"Next Tuesday. Thank you, Hammy." She turned away obediently into the crowd, adjusting the strap of her large shoulder bag. Hammond watched her disappear.

CHAPTER NINE

"APPLE, APPLE HONEY, Apple," Billy said, switching the lead rope to his other hand. "Your hands are too high, your heels are up, what are you doing, for God's sake?"

Apple's hands came down on the saddle, she lowered her heels, but she was still tilted forward like a mechanical bird, bobbing with each of the pony's strides.

"Sit back and relax," Billy said, from the center of the ring she was describing on the pony. He flicked his long whip, and the pony jerked his head and picked up his feet.

"I don't feel like relaxing," Apple said.

"I know you don't feel like relaxing. Right now you're probably mad as hell. It's hot, your rear end hurts, and you want to quit and go home and have you a nice warm bath."

"Yes," Apple said.

Billy flicked the whip again, and the pony lumbered into a trot. Apple bounced high and squealed. "Sit back," Billy said, laughing. "You want to lose your maidenhead?"

"Don't talk that way!" Apple shouted. She continued to bounce up and down as the pony turned on the end of Billy's lead rope. Billy noticed after a while that she was biting her lip and realized that she had passed, quickly, as she so often did, from irritation to tears. He wondered what he had touched.

"I want you to canter, sit back, and canter," he said, touching up the pony, who scampered for a stride or two and then broke into a rolling gait. Apple pitched forward on the pony's neck, scrabbled with her hands, and lost a stirrup. She was sliding to one side. Billy stood his ground, clucking to the pony. Apple dragged herself back into the saddle and turned to him, her face flaming. "I don't want to do this anymore!"

"I know, but I want you to. We agreed."

"I used to love to ride when I could do it the way I wanted to do it!"

"Sloppy as hell, heels in the air, looking like a fool."

"I don't care what I looked like!" But she sat back and caught the rhythm.

"Well, I care. I'm going to take you to Lexington, get you a well-cut riding jacket, pair of decent britches — none of those blue jeans — maybe even a tattersall vest, if you're good."

"Who's going to pay for all of that?"

"I expect you're going to have to, Miss Apple. Certainly if you want to get yourself a pair of handmade boots. They will cost you a good deal more than I could afford," he said, sighing.

"Why do I have to have so much money?" she grumbled.

"We'll talk about that one time when you aren't canter-ing," he said, touched by her embarrasment.

He'd thought money was only his problem: his lack of it, his yearning for it. But it was Apple's problem, too: she had too much. He wondered if she'd begun to notice that even money might not staunch their yearning. They would buy things together, they would live well, but was either of them capable of being comfortable — or comforted?

"Time to stop," he said, drawing in the lead rope, ap-proaching the pony slowly; he settled down to a walk, blow-ing, his side wet with sweat stains. "There, old boy." He stroked his neck. "Fat as an old plug! He isn't so bad. He's getting the idea."

"I love him," Apple said, leaning forward and kissing the pony on his neck. "I've had him since I was twelve years old and now you go and call him a plug. He's got some quarter horse in him."

"I don't know where." Billy held up his arms, and Apple, dropping the reins, slid off into them. She leaned against his shoulder, tipped her chin up, and stared at the fading, soft blue sky.

"We've been out here all afternoon. I'm so tired I could die."

"Yes. I worked you."

"I've lost five pounds since you started on me. Mother is worrying."

"She'll worry more before I'm through with you," Billy said. "Here, take your reins, don't just turn your mount loose."

With the pony clopping behind them, they walked to the

barn. Going up the hill, they crossed Mrs. Mason's prize lawn, and Billy looked down at the hoof marks the pony was leaving. "We'll have us a regular path through here, before long."

"Yes, I expect so. Mother will be furious. She never lets me ride this near the house — I mean, she never used to let me."

"Seems to me it's time for those rules to change."

Apple said, "I do pretty much what I want."

"I've noticed that. The rules stay the rules, but Miss Apple gets away with murder."

"You always have me home by eleven o'clock."

"That's only because I have to get up early to go to work."

Apple slid her hand inside Billy's arm. The pony, behind them, fluffed a breath that lifted the edges of Apple's hair. "Aren't you attracted to me?" she asked in a low voice.

"Everybody's attracted to you, Apple. Have been since the day you started nursery school."

"I'm talking about you."

"I'm as attracted as anybody else. It doesn't matter."

"It matters to me. Don't you want to touch me?" She took hold of his right hand, by the fingers, and laid it inside her jacket, on her small breast. "Don't you like to touch that?"

Billy snatched his hand out. "In my own good time," he said, breathlessly.

"Yeah, you like that," she said, watching him.

"You want to get it over with so you can go on to someone else," he said, angry at last. "That's been the story of your life — don't interrupt! You get whoever the new man is and suck him dry and fling his carcass on the heap —"

"I don't expect you to believe me, but I am a virgin," Apple said in a stately voice.

Billy glanced at her bowed head, the blond hair hiding her profile. Apple did not usually lie. She answered with jokes, or with silence, or with what Billy knew were the closest approximations she possessed to the truth. Still, he was certain that now she was lying, and he wondered what pressure was forcing her in that unnatural direction.

"I don't expect you to believe me," he said in his turn, "but I don't care whether or not you're a virgin —" He stopped and thought, Is that true? I can't afford to care, he decided. It's too late to try to justify everything she's done.

"Once I made out in a car with some guy and he touched me between my legs."

"I don't want to hear about it."

"Well, that's nothing — you know that," Apple said lightly. "Some other guy tried to kiss my breasts —"

"I don't want to hear about it!"

"OK." She smiled. "I thought you didn't believe in jealousy."

"I never told you that." He slipped the reins from her hand and led the pony into the cool, damp barn. He snatched off the saddle and began to brush his sweaty side. "Get the currycomb. You can do his mane."

Apple fetched the metal comb and began to plow through the pony's topknot. "Do you believe in jealousy?" she asked, after a calming moment.

"It's not something you believe or disbelieve in. It's something you know. Something you feel. If I love a woman, I'm jealous — it's as simple as that. I don't want her to do the things with me she does with some other man.'

144

"What things?" Apple asked, cautious now, approaching the core. She combed a burr out of the pony's mane and threw it down. "The trouble is, Billy, if we're going steady —"

"That's not what I call it."

"If we're dating —"

"Not that either."

"Well, keeping company, then!"

"Better."

"If that's what we're doing, we have to agree about jealousy. That's the first thing we have to agree about, wouldn't you say? Not to trip each other up?"

"We can't agree on it because it's beyond agreement." He was leaning down to brush the pony's white stockings, and his voice sounded congested. "Look, if you see somebody you want to go to bed with, you're going to do it, Apple, and no agreement we have will make the slightest difference."

"What about you?"

"I don't work that way. It's more complicated."

"But remember, I'm a virgin," she said.

"Apple, don't lie." Now he was staring at her over the pony's back.

"Why would I lie?"

"Because you think it's what I want to hear."

"Is it?"

Billy looked at her with irritation. "Yes," he said. "Of course it's what I want to hear."

"Well, then, you see —"

"No, I don't see." He took the currycomb out of her hand and began to saw it through the pony's mane. "You don't make up fables to please me any more than you cook brownies to please me or curl your hair or put on lipstick. I'm all the time after you to spruce up! And here you tell me you lie to please me when you won't do any of those other things."

"Those other things are boring," Apple said. "Are we going to turn him out in the pasture?"

"Apple," Billy said suddenly, "I love you. I want to comb your pony's mane and argue with you for the rest of my life."

"It's hardly an argument," she said lightly, slipping the halter over the pony's head. "At most it's a difference of opinion."

"Did you hear what I said?" He grabbed her hand and held it, hard, the buckle of the halter inside her palm. "Were you listening at all?"

"I heard some kind of nonsense. Let me go, I want to fasten this thing."

"You'll believe me, by and by," he said grimly. "You'll have to."

"Don't you think you should try me, first?" She was leading the pony out to the gate, and she spoke to Billy over her shoulder. "Don't you think you should see whether or not I suit, in bed?"

"Oh, quit that. This isn't a bargain basement." He followed along behind, noticing her long, lean thighs. She was made for expensive riding clothes.

"I'm not going to believe a word you say till you try me," Apple said. "After all, we live in the seventies, not in some ancient time. Sometimes you sound like my mother!"

Billy laughed. "There are worse things. I have some kind of creeping respect for your mother."

"I wouldn't say she has any kind of respect, creeping or not, for you." Apple crashed the gate behind the pony and Billy. "There! Trapped!" she said, sliding the chain around the post and closing the padlock.

"Idiot." He put his boot on the lowest board of the gate, then stopped. "I don't think I'll climb over."

"Well then, you'll have to sit there and stew," she said, stepping back and poking her hands into her pockets.

"Open the gate, Apple."

"Not unless you agree to do anything I want!"

"Open the gate!"

"Why should I?" She giggled. "So you can lecture me?"

Billy did not reply. He looked around for somewhere to sit. There was a stump, farther back, in the heaven tree thicket where the old pony stood, head down, flicking his tail at flies. Billy turned and sauntered off. Apple, at the gate, called, "Where are you going?"

He sat down on the stump with his back to her, facing down the hill. The mulberry tree in the valley was covered with fruit; birds rose and fell among its limbs, chirping. Underneath the tree, an old bathtub waited, full of water. The pony came up behind Billy, snuffled in his shoulder, blew, and sagged off down the hill to drink. He watched him drop his head into the tub, pulling water up as powerfully as a pump. Watching, he wondered how long Apple was going to make him wait.

"Bil-ly!" she called, softly, wheedling. "Getting late, Bil-ly!"

147

"As soon as you unlock the gate," he said, taking a pack of cigarettes out of his pocket and lighting one. He cocked one knee over the other, leaned forward, inhaling, and watched the pony drink.

"You've got to give me something before I let you out!" Apple called. He heard the chain rattle as she climbed on the gate.

"What do you want?" He did not lift his voice or turn his head, but she heard him.

"Many things!" she called in a soft, singsong voice as though she was a mother reading a fairy tale. Billy remembered hearing somewhere that girls are fashioned in some way by the fairy tales they read. "Many things!" Apple repeated in her silver, artificial voice. "Grant me my wish, oh prince!"

Billy sat silent. He could feel her studying his back from the gate.

"What do you want, Apple?" he asked, after a while.

"Tell me the truth," she said, sharply. "Were you in love with my sister Corinne?"

Billy felt for the automatic denial, then let it slip. Silence stretched between them. Down the hill, the pony finished drinking, pulled his head out of the tub, slipped back his lips, and yawned.

"Yes," Billy said. He leaned down and put the cigarette out in the dust at his feet.

He heard the chain rattling as he stood up. Apple swung open the gate. Coming towards her, he looked at her as though for the first time. She was leaning on the gate, waiting to close it; evading his eyes, she glanced down the valley and said, "The pony's rolling." They turned to look at the pony, belly up, legs flailing. "My, that must feel good on those horsefly bites,' Apple said.

Billy put his arm around her. She stood in the half embrace, looking away over his shoulder. "Corinne wouldn't have me," Billy said.

"Why not?"

He took hold of her chin and turned her head. "She wanted to get out of here," he said.

"She told you that?"

"She didn't need to tell me; anybody could have seen it from the way she acted at those deb parties. Like a visitor from another planet, observing the barbarian rites. Kind, polite, so detached it was a surprise to feel how warm her hand was when I danced with her."

"She didn't want to make her debut. She did it to please Mother."

"Whatever. Anyway, she did let me get close to her, once —" He hesitated. Apple looked away. "But then she told me, right away, that it wasn't going to work the way I wanted it to work, that she couldn't agree to see me anymore. She was leaving in a week, and she didn't plan to be home much after that. She was so clear. You know, it was the first time I'd met a girl as clear as that" — he remembered the sensation of Corinne's clearness — "and of course I had to admire that."

"You wanted her," Apple said, looking away, trying to accustom herself to the idea.

He kissed her neck. "Yes, Apple, I wanted her. In the worst way." He forced himself that far. "She was — is, I guess — very pretty."

"No," Apple said. "She's beautiful. Cory is beautiful. I am pretty."

"Yes," he said, after a while. "You're right."

She turned away and began to walk down the road. He followed. It seemed to him that she had never appeared in such a good light. He had resisted throwing too many kinds of light on her because she was, after all, only nineteen years old, spoiled, protected, pretty, and he did not want — would never want — to see through her. Now she shone, opaque, against the strong yellow light of his memory of Corinne.

"Corinne always gets everything first," Apple said, without bitterness. "She started going to parties first. She started collecting boys first. She was supposed to be the first woman in our family to go to college. Of course she was the first to get married . . ." Apple sighed. "I love Cory," she said, "but sometimes it's hard not to hold her firstness against her."

Billy laughed. "You know, that's just what I wouldn't have been able to stand . . . "

"You mean, it's my secondness —"

"Apple, I'm a second. In more ways than one. We might as well both agree to that while we still can. I don't have anything your other — beaux — have. I don't have money or looks or position. All I have is hopes. Corinne would have outshone me to such a degree —"

"And I don't."

She was walking fast, hurrying along.

"I hope someday you will," he said, meaning it, yet also aware of the fact that he was safe.

"I don't like us to match that way," Apple said, ignoring his flattery. "I like us to match in a bigger way. By our strengths — something like that."

"You and I still have to grow our strengths." They were passing a hedge of wild roses, and Billy stopped Apple and broke off a bloom. He tucked its stem into a buttonhole at the neck of her shirt. "There. Pretty!" he said, giving the word, he hoped, a new gloss.

Apple looked at him blankly. Then she reached up and touched the pink rose with her forefinger. "It's like a baby's mouth," she said. "We will have babies, won't we?"

She sounded so wistful Billy laughed. "Of course we will, silly. Dozens of them."

She was not amused. "Now I understand why you don't want to sleep with me."

Billy sighed. "Look, it has more to do with you and me —"

"No," she said, starting down the road again. "It has more to do with you and Cory."

"I told you why that didn't work."

"But you must have thought, somehow, that it would have worked if you hadn't been so . . ."

"Impetuous?"

"Yes."

"I don't think that would have altered a thing." But he wondered, and she knew it. She continued on down the road as though she was alone, walking fast, looking at the toes of her stubbed leather boots. Billy hurried along beside her, feeling the distance between them, wanting to bridge it with something more substantial than his hand on her elbow. She might knock that off, in any event. They walked past the old rope swing, hanging lopsided, where once he had pushed her until her toes touched the maple. They passed the formal flower garden, set between four concrete urns, and saw a splash of yellow — Apple's mother, bending down to weed. They went along until the house came in sight, against its grove of magnolias, and still Billy could not find a way to bridge the gap. He decided to give it up, for the moment, to let her sulk (if she was sulking) and to hope that after a bath, a change, a drink, and dinner downtown she might fade for a little into his arms, sitting outside the house in his Dodge with the night noises loud around them. He would feel her breast, if it would reassure her, tell her (if only he could) that her tiny pink nipples — which he had only seen through her white shirts — were prettier than Corinne's larger, darker ones. More beautiful.

At the door, she turned, the knob in her hand, and asked, "Do you want to come in?"

"Of course!"

As she led the way into the cool, black-and-white tiled hall, she said, "I lied to you, anyway."

"Yes?"

"I'm not a virgin."

"I knew, silly." But he felt a pang.

CHAPTER TEN

C ORINNE PUT BUDDY on the train for the city Monday morning and then gave herself up to the summer. It was already hot — eight o'clock, a deep blue sky, and the maples along the two-lane road from the broken-down Hudson River station were full of rustling light. A hot day was predicted on the radio between sections of music. She scuffed off her shoes and drove barefooted, feeling the rubber ridges in the accelerator pedal and the brake.

She stopped at the A & P in town and went down the aisle with a little basket on her arm, collecting her kind of food: fruit, cheese, a few cans of bouillon, a lot of fruit juice. She expected to spend five days alone, her expectation hovering on the brink of fear. She would spend five days alone if. She would spend five days alone unless. Buddy would telephone on Tuesday and again on Thursday, and on Friday she would go down to meet his train. In between, she was free.

Freedom was not something that took up much space,

and it shimmered and slid, into the bargain. She wondered if she had been vulgar all along, in her heart, even when she was serving Buddy's guests at her little dinner parties in the city (silver shined, pepper mill filled, a bunch of fresh flowers in the middle of the table), even when she had been listening to records with him, hours on end silent in the face of Bach, even when they had strolled, on late winter afternoons, down Park Avenue and seen the buildings near Grand Central Station glowing with early lights.

Perhaps, she thought, it's the country that's done it, brought out my piggishness, made me want to go whole hog.

She carried her bag of groceries to the car, speaking on the way to Mrs. Dawson, an inquisitive lady who ran the bookstore. "I've got that book you ordered, that poetry," she said, and Corinne realized that she had forgotten the title.

"Forget about it, Mrs. Dawson. I don't want it anymore," she said, climbing into the car and then, seeing the woman's surprised face, she rolled down her window and added, "I'm sorry, I'm very sorry, I guess I changed my mind." But she was not sorry, and her mind was not changed. It was revealed.

She drove out of town, past the twin white farmhouses built, the previous century, by a devoted pair of brothers, past the raw earth where the new Baptist home was going up. She turned the radio louder and tapped the accelerator to the beat: "Red Sails in the Sunset." She swung up Violet Road and drove between high banks under drooping maples, their trunks twined with honeysuckle, awash in a sea

of sumac, past the neighbor's farm where the Black Angus
were moving slowly up the hill to their place in the shade
near the top. "I love it here," Corinne said, aloud, "I love
it, I love it," and pressed down hard on the accelerator with
her bare foot, springing the car across the intersection in
front of a tractor, plodding along, glaring with its insect
headlights.

At the house, she hopped out and carried her bag into
the big, sunny, dirty kitchen. There were crumbs on the
floor and spiderwebs in the corners of the ceiling which had
thickened with a coating of grease. Buddy now and then
suggested that she find a cleaning woman, but Corinne did
not like the idea of having a stranger in the house. She would
whisk a broom around, now and then, flip a dust rag, and
once she had gone down on her knees to scrub the sallow
linoleum. That could not be a regular thing. The house was
crowded and cheerful, and she could find anything she
wanted, a book, a piece of knitting, without having to wonder first where she had put it away; it was a small house,
her house, bought out of the estate her grandmother had
left her, and she took some satisfaction in the fact that all
of Buddy's things were confined to a little rickety gateleg
table in the bathroom: his shaving soap and brush and razor
and his bottle of expensive after-shave lotion. In the city,
Buddy had a library, a desk, and several closets full of
clothes.

She sat down at the table to drink a cup of coffee; it was
cold, but that didn't matter. She poured in some of Mrs.
Cheshire's milk, fetched twice a week from the dairy in the
valley, and watched the grease gleam on the surface of the

coffee. It did not seem to matter what happened next. She thought vaguely of reading or listening to the radio or knitting away on the long pale thing that might develop into an arm for a sweater. Then she felt the sun hot on her back as it moved across the window and thought that the best thing would be to get undressed and go for a swim.

She went upstairs, dropped her clothes on the floor, and tied on a terry-cloth robe.

Stepping out along the fieldstone path, she thanked heaven for the pool: deep, small, like a measuring cup filled with dark green water.

She stepped up onto the cement edge, dropped her robe off her shoulders, and dove in. She parted the water with her hands, five feet down; it was dark when she opened her eyes. Streaming bubbles, her long hair flowing behind her, she swam through the water, holding her breath, her arms at her sides. She turned at the shallow end and started back and made it all the way, coming up with a burst of water, gasping for air. She had learned to swim underwater as a child, and it still seemed more comfortable than splashing along on the surface.

Rolling out of the pool, she lay dripping and panting on the wet cement. The water from her hair ran down her back and begin to dry in the sun. She slipped her hand under her belly and pressed the swell around her navel, feeling her vagina move; she longed for the feeling of a baby in her womb and found that her sensations focused there, feeding the hungriness, making her belly sensitive. She groaned, pressed against her hand, grinding her knuckles into the cement.

From the house, the telephone began to ring. She flipped over on her back, squinting up at the sky. There was no one to call her — she had no friends. After it had rung four or five times, she realized that whoever it was was not going to give up, and she stood up, slipped her robe on, and started for the house. It occurred to her that it might be Peter, yet she did not hurry. The best, she thought, was now: the blessed anticipation, which belonged to her, which she did not need to share.

It was the Seventh-Day Adventists, asking for a contribution. She dropped the telephone back onto its cradle.

Opening the refrigerator, she took out a pitcher of orange juice and poured herself a glass. She swallowed it all down, then turned back to the pool. It was only nine o'clock; the whole day, the whole blessed early summer day stretched in front of her, unmarred by a single obligation. She even had food in the house.

The next time the telephone rang, she let it go, although she knew it must be Peter. She lay on her belly on the warm cement and dozed.

Later, she heard a car turn into the gravel drive, spitting bits of stone from its wheels; she did not open her eyes. She heard the car door bang, then feet along the path to the house, heard his hard hammering on the screen door. "Corinne! Corinne!" She giggled, pressed her face into her hands, wondered how long it would take him to find her. It did not seem to matter: it did not even seem to matter if he missed her altogether and stormed off in the station wagon.

"There you are," Peter said from the rise, and she giggled

157

and flattened herself against the cement. He came crashing down the steps, knocked a geranium aside, and strode over to her; then he kneeled down, peeled her hand back, and stared at her face. "You dirty thing, you were hiding," he said, "lying out here naked!" Then he kissed her shoulder, the middle of her back, and the line where her thigh met her buttock. Corinne shivered and turned over.

He looked around at the fields and said, "Let's go inside."

"How come?"

"Is it safe here?"

"Nobody ever comes."

But she stood up, put on her robe, and started towards the house.

"So you're not shy?" he said, following her. "I thought from the way you winced when I kissed your nipple the other night you might be shy."

"It wasn't the other night, it was Saturday night," she said. "How many women have you kissed in between?"

"None, in the nipple," he said.

Inside the kitchen, she turned and put her arms around him and studied him seriously. "I want you to love me, Peter," she said. "Love me, love me, love me."

"I want to screw you," he said, feeling for her hips.

"Yes, that too, but it's got to be love."

"I don't know about that," he said, sliding his hand through her robe, between her thighs. "You're all wet. Let's talk about love later."

She moved slowly against his hand, but she did not take her eyes off his face. "It won't work for me unless you love me," she said. "I know that. That's why it's never worked for me with Buddy. He tries, but he can't love me, it's not in him."

He was pressing his thumb into her vagina. "Don't you take some responsibility?"

"No," she said, tilting her pelvis, making it easier for him. "I don't take any responsibility at all."

"Why not?" he asked, holding his thumb rigid for her.

"Because I know what I can do when I'm loved," she said, arching forward, kissing his neck. "Come on. Let's go upstairs."

He followed her. She could hear his shoes slap on the bare wooden steps. The little gabled bedroom was filled with light, and the rocking chair moved slightly on the rag rug as they entered; the white bed, unmade, was a tossed sea of pillows. Corinne lay down and opened her robe. "Come on," she said. He took off his shoes and socks, and sat down on the edge of the bed to unbutton his shirt. She leaned down over him and began to unbutton it for him, kissing his smooth, hairless chest. "I've found you," she said. "I've found you, I'm not going to let you go."

"Is this a game?" he asked.

She put her hand on his penis. "You're hard."

He lay back. She unzipped his fly. Then she whooped, laughed, and set herself astride him.

$\mathcal{M}$R. MASON came up at eleven-thirty with his umbrella in his hand and his hat on his head to fetch Billy for the errand. He stood for a while in the corridor outside Billy's office while the young man finished dictating a letter. Billy had wanted to interrupt the letter, but Mr. Mason had said that was out of the question. Their appointment wasn't until noon, and the letter, regardless of its nature, must be handled first.

They went down in the elevator together, Mr. Mason standing soberly, his feet apart, the tip of the umbrella planted between his toes, while Billy leaned an elbow on the green wall and chatted with Pinky, the elevator attendant, an ancient negro man.

"Hot," Pinky said, feeling the back of his neck with a skinny hand. "Look like this time of year, fall coming, this heat would break for sure."

"We're going to have a thunderstorm later on, according to the paper," Mr. Mason said soothingly as Pinky shot back the gilded doors.

"Sure enough, Mr. Ham, sure enough."

They passed through the revolving door into the hot breath of Main Street: the concrete burned through the soles of their shoes with the summer's accumulated heat, and at the crossing, a small crowd of bedraggled shoppers seemed to be leaning on the thick air. As they crossed, Billy glanced from habit at the big white-faced clock across the river, and Mr. Mason said proudly, "Second biggest clock in the world, after Big Ben. I said when I took my wife to London, it gave me a queer kind of satisfaction to think at home we have that big clock's nearest kin."

"River's up," Billy said, inconsequentially; he did not want to enter into bragging about the town.

"Yes, they had rain in the east earlier this week. The way they're cutting trees, we get whole mountains dissolved and floating downstream."

They crossed and started up Third, past three parking lots and the massive red brick facade of Levy's Department Store. The windows were showing fall fashions on feature-less mannequins: "Could be boys or girls," Mr. Mason observed, adding, "That store's been in one family for five generations. I used to buy my clothes there, but they've been cutting corners and you can't find anything that doesn't have some kind of synthetic in it. Even underwear." Billy understood that he had hoisted a flag of intimacy, and laughed.

"I get my clothes wherever I can find them, which is I guess mainly Stewarts."

"Well, that's not bad," Mr. Mason said with the same reassuring note Billy had caught when they spoke to Pinky. He wondered if he looked that unsure.

Mr. Mason matched him stride for stride as they swung up Third, crossing Walnut, passing quickly along the glaring glass facades of a couple of empty bars. Mr. Mason drew a white linen handkerchief out of his pocket and passed it rapidly across his forehead. "In my father's day, this sort of thing would have been closed up in twenty-four hours. The police knew whose opinions they were supposed to respect. But we're so much freer now."

"I've been in some of these places. They're all right."

"I don't mean I expect everybody to pay his homage to whiskey at the Pendennis Club."

"I kind of like this ratty side of town."

"Well, I know what you mean. It has a life. I mean, after all, Times Square has a life, too. But when I think of visitors coming here, seeing this. . . . This town has got to pull itself together, one of these days. Get a first-class team of architects in, do something about this street — you know, they're trying malls in the East, paving the streets, putting in trees and so forth. It makes a very attractive place to shop. And safe!"

"I like it the way it is," Billy said, enjoying his flash of stubbornness.

They turned briskly down Chestnut — Billy felt marched along — and strode through the revolving door into the long, dark main floor of Stewarts. Big fans on top of the counters stirred the air. The noontime crowd of lady shoppers was already surging around piles of reduced nylon underwear in pastel shades and an enormous heap of cast-off sunglasses.

"Adeline asked us to meet them on the third floor," Mr. Mason said.

Following in his wake, Billy saw him nod and speak to several of the older women, felt the hush which followed him.

He wondered how many of the shoppers were actually in Mr. Mason's debt for a job, a recommendation, a word to the right person, and how many were merely impressed — swept away, rather — by the possibilities Mr. Mason represented of a life lived on a larger order. It was as though he had tickets in his pockets for all the big cities in the world. Billy appreciated that, he realized, more than the ability to confer or withhold favors: the flavor of a foreignness, of sophistication, which was acquired, like a hard shine on silver, only after years of remorseless application.

They stood single file on the escalator and, glancing in the mirror, Billy thought with amusement that they looked as matched, in their dark suits, as a pair of tin soldiers.

He could not guess what Apple would think of his suitability — she had only seen him with her father a couple of times — and he nearly pushed ahead of Mr. Mason in his eagerness to see the expression on her face. Mr. Mason, however, kept a firm lead, and they went on as they were, single file, Billy almost treading on the older man's heels, into a pale blue room at the back of the ladies' clothing floor.

A fake window, gauzed in white, seemed to look out on a painted garden, brilliantly lit from below. Mr. Mason, as though stopped by the brilliance, hesitated, and Billy bumped into him and apologized. A small, spidery woman, dressed in black, came scurrying towards them; she was wringing her hands, or clapping them — it was hard to distinguish. "We're just getting started!" she cried in a thin voice, glancing from Billy's face to Mr. Mason's. "Just now, just now getting started! She forgot to bring her pumps — of course we were prepared for that — so much excitement! — and I went down to Ladies' Better Shoes to bring her up a pair."

"Why, what did she have on her feet?" Mr. Mason asked.

"Nothing but an old pair of canvas tennis shoes," the woman said, suddenly descending to practicality. Billy saw an oblong card pinned to her straight bosom and read it with relief: "Miss Henrietta."

"Miss Henrietta, I'd like you to meet Billy Long," Mr. Mason said, stepping away from between them.

Miss Henrietta rushed into the gap, seized Billy's hand, and wrung it with both her own. "The happy man!" she cried.

Mr. Mason winked at Billy over the top of Miss Henrietta's head. "Well, I've been very lucky, and that's a fact," Billy told Miss Henrietta solemnly.

She interrupted him with a gale of cajolery. "Luck! When has luck ever entered into it? Why, I have only to look at you . . . " And so forth. Mr. Mason winked again, and Billy felt sustained by their shared merriment.

"Where is my wife?" Mr. Mason asked after a while, interrupting the stream.

"Oh, excuse me! Here I am keeping you both waiting when what you want is to see the girls." She fluttered off, and Mr. Mason nodded at one of the blue tufted sofas, saying, "Think you can bear to sit down?"

"We better. It looks like it's going to be a long one."

They sat together, tentatively, their hands on their knees.

The pale blue sofa, squeezed, exhaled a small weary breath which smelled of talcum powder.

Miss Henrietta hurried back, followed by Mrs. Mason. She was wearing a hat, a small pink saucer, with a scrap of veil, tilted coquettishly over one eye, and Billy, snapping to attention, meant it when he said, "Mrs. Mason, you are looking particularly fine."

She disparaged that and gave her husband a kiss. Billy had never seen them kiss before, and he was surprised by the sound their lips made. He wondered if his kisses and Apple's would be as long lasting. Certainly there was too much tearing and rending now. That, of course, would pass; she would begin to open her mouth as daintily as her mother, who looked as though she expected a gumdrop to slide between her carefully parted lips. Billy realized with a start that the old people were still having sex together. Still! But surely that, too, was a good sign.

Miss Henrietta conducted them back to the sofa. She seemed apprehensive about their remaining on their feet. Once they were seated, she stood over them, clasping her hands, ready to give commands. Mr. and Mrs. Mason had settled to one side, and Billy found himself alone on the loveseat, which faced the pink-draped door to the dressing room.

"She will be out in a moment — just a moment! I have Libby in there, down on her knees . . ." She lifted the pink curtain and passed through.

"It really is a sweet dress," Mrs. Mason said into their shared silence. "I'm not the least bit sorry, now, that we didn't insist on ordering it in New York."

"Apple being so determined not to miss a single riding lesson —" Mr. Mason smiled at Billy.

"Of course I would have excused her for a trip to New York —"

"She did not want to be excused," Mr. Mason said. "You will find — probably have found already — that my younger daughter takes, or makes, her own excuses."

"Up in the heat this morning to go out and exercise that pony," Mrs. Mason said. "I told her you wouldn't expect it when you two were out so late last night." She looked at him, one eye veiled, the other unobstructed, shining.

"We went swimming in that old quarry up at the Websters'." He saw them waiting, hanging on his words, yet could not bring himself to describe the mossy, dark, silent water into which Apple, dressed in a cotton bra and childish underpants, had plunged, straight down, coming up only after he had despaired, all the way at the other side of the quarry.

"Those old quarries!" Mrs. Mason said, to make up for his reticence. "You have to be careful in those old quarries! People have drowned there."

"Not recently, Adeline,' Mr. Mason said, patting her hand.

"I didn't think Apple took her bathing suit when you went out to dinner . . . "

"She swam in her underwear. I didn't swim at all," Billy added, wondering why that seemed to make a difference. In fact, he would have gone a long way to avoid throwing himself into that dark water.

"Apple is so energetic," Mrs. Mason remarked, apparently because of the swimming. "How do you think that will wear, in a wife?"

In spite of her flirtatious smile, Billy knew that she expected a direct answer.

"She's going to take some curbing," he said.

They both looked at him.

"I don't mean anything severe," he went on calmly. "I just mean it'll be part of my job to channel that enthusiasm, make sure it goes into something worthwhile."

"I believe you are going to have your job cut out for you," Mr. Mason said.

His wife explained, "You see, Apple likes the energy itself. I don't believe she really cares much what it is used for."

"Then my job will be to teach her." He was glad to lay it out on the table.

They were silent. Mrs. Mason poked in her purse and Mr. Mason drove the tip of his umbrella into the pale blue carpet.

And then, with Miss Henrietta beating time with her hands, Apple came through the pink-draped door. She was wearing a long white dress, which she gathered up in front with both hands so that she could stride towards them. Billy saw her tan legs and thought of the long thigh muscles which she used to effect now against the pony's sides. He saw a piece of lace over her breasts, oddly shaped — a parallelogram — and long white sleeves that came down in points to her knuckles. She stopped, twirled, demanded that Billy count the buttons on her back. He did not move from his seat. Mrs. Mason stood up and went to her daughter and touched the top button and said, "Darling, you have

exactly the same number I had, it's the number for brides —
don't ask me why, I don't believe there is a reason."

"Sixty buttons for sixty years!" Miss Henrietta cried.

Mrs. Mason looked amused. "Is that really it?"

"That is really it," Miss Henrietta replied. "Now if you
are all ready, we will try the veil."

She led Apple, who looked back, winking at Billy, to a
draped stand in the middle of the room. Then she started
to help Apple up onto the stand, a hand under her elbow.
Apple jumped up, planted her feet, and turned around
jauntily, her hands on her hips. Miss Henrietta reverently
opened a large white box and took out a piece of veil, yellow
with age. She laid the veil over her forearm and carried it
to Apple. Mrs. Mason was saying, "My great-grandmother's
veil, Billy. She wore it at her wedding in the eighteen
eighties."

Miss Henrietta stood on tiptoe beside the platform and
laid the veil on the top of Apple's head. The veil settled,
she drew herself up to her full height, and shot at the three
lookers-on a glance full of impudence and spite. "Great-
grandmother's underwear — that's what I'd like to see!
Laces up the front and pink roses . . . "

"Granny Morton would never have had anything to do
with pink roses," Mrs. Mason said reprovingly. "What do
you think, Henrietta — a little higher?" She went to the dais
and, touching Apple's shoulder, brought her down to the
right height. Then she carefully rearranged the veil on her
daughter's hair.

Apple, straightening, looked chastened.

Mr. Mason leaned over and said to Billy, "Now you're

seeing her looking as bridey as she'll ever look. I hope it'll do."

"It'll do."

"I'm going to run an errand, and then we'll meet for lunch," Mr. Mason said. "Downstairs. Will you get a table and hold it? There's a mob in the cafeteria at lunchtime." He stood up.

Billy stood up at the same time. "I'll go down there now."

Mrs. Mason was speaking to Miss Henrietta. Apple frowned at her father and Billy. "You two going off somewhere?"

"We'll leave you to finish," Mr. Mason said. He went to his daughter, touched her arm inside the tight satin sleeve, and kissed her cheek. He had to stand on tiptoe. Billy, aware suddenly of the discrepancy in their heights, decided to forgo his kiss. He waved at Apple and made his way towards the door.

"Order me a cheeseburger!" she shouted after him. "Blood raw. And French fries!"

"It's women's work, always has been," Mr. Mason said as they started towards the elevator. "I know they'll get finished with it faster without us there. When Cory was married, they went on this way for three months. Of course that was the first. I think Adeline's resigned to a few short-cuts, this time: two kinds of oysters instead of three at the reception, for instance."

"Is Corinne coming down for the wedding?"

Silence welled between them. Finally, choosing candor, Mr. Mason said, "No, I don't believe so. She hasn't been well." With the tip of his umbrella, he pressed the elevator call button. "Of course, with Cory, you never know. She might change her mind . . ." He glanced at Billy.

"I know what you mean," Billy said.

"I'm sorry, to tell you the truth, that she won't be here. It seems sad. The girls have always been unusually close. But there's trouble, up there — I won't go into it; they have to get through it their own way." Mr. Mason seemed to be waiting for a question, but Billy held his peace.

They stepped into the crowded elevator, and Mr. Mason nodded and smiled to several acquaintances. Billy, facing front, wondered how long it would be before he knew faces in every crowd. It was a pleasant prospect. He smelled the perfume of the woman beside him and looked at the lobe of her right ear and wondered whether knowing her name would eliminate the mild erotic curiosity he felt about her now; would she become, in a few years, merely Mrs. Benson Straight (or whatever) rather than a pretty dark-haired stranger wearing Nuit D'Amour?

They stepped out on the ground floor, Mr. Mason standing aside to let the women surge past. "I'm going to Perfume. My secretary's birthday is tomorrow, and I'm going to get her something — a little Blue Grass spray, I think. I like her to wear a scent I'm fond of since we're closed up together all day long." He rolled his eyes at Billy. "You know Miss Weaver?"

"Yes. If you'd like my opinion, I'd say the Blue Grass spray would be perfect."

"She's been wearing it for seventeen years," Mr. Mason said. "I'll meet you downstairs in the cafeteria."

Billy rode the escalator down and walked through Housewares, noticing a row of copper pans and making a note to suggest to Apple that she add the pans to their gift list. In front of him, the doorway to the cafeteria was wreathed in pale green painted vines. A sign, ivy-framed, announced the name: Garden Place. He went in and stood near the cashier, searching for a table. The place was already filling up with shoppers — women in pairs, carrying bags and purses and looking for places to leave their coats and umbrellas.

He had to ask a waitress's help to find a table that would seat four. Everything except the counter was arranged for pairs, and he knew Mr. Mason would not accept the counter. Then he sat down at the table and ordered a cup of coffee.

Women, sitting alone, edged the sides of the room on red benches while the couples took up the center space. Billy felt rather conspicuous. Men normally ate across the street at The Colonnade.

Near him, two women were chatting over their garden salads. Their voices calmed him, reminding him of his mother's sweetness, of the rare meals they had shared "outside," when she had taken it upon herself to amuse him with anecdotes spun out of the dim stuff of her life: jokes from telephone conversations, tiffs among her friends, all embroidered and colored up to catch his attention. It seemed a womanly gift. He hoped Apple would acquire it.

"They say they're getting married in two weeks," a woman sitting nearby, a sparrow-like creature in a brown feathered hat, was remarking to her friend. "You'd think with all that hoopla, they'd wait longer than three weeks between the announcement and the wedding."

"They do things faster, these days." Her friend, a slender young woman with long straight blond hair, broke a cracker in two and ate a half delicately.

"Well, I still say it's strange. They'll want to do everything the right way — you know *her*. She's a stickler for details if ever there was one. And then rushing the time between the announcement and the wedding. It's enough to make anybody wonder."

"It doesn't make me wonder," the younger woman said, beginning on her salad.

"Well, you're just too young and innocent, that's all."

Billy's attention, turning slowly like a weather vane in a drifting breeze, fixed itself on the two women. He looked at them surreptitiously.

The older woman was nearly his mother's age although she had preserved a girlish prettiness which matched her soft feathered hat. He could see her neat feet, crossed at the ankle, and the abundant curve of her hip. Her friend was skinny by comparison and he wondered at the disparity in their ages; perhaps they were related — aunt and niece.

"I think the least we can do is wish them every possible happiness," the younger woman went on, giving her aunt a meaningful glance.

The older woman considered. "I don't want to sound mean-spirited, but those people have everything. Money. Position. Looks. It goes against human nature to wish them happy marriages into the bargain." She smiled at her niece. "It goes against my human nature, at least. I don't know about yours."

"You talk that way because you've never met them. I went

to school with Apple Mason. We were in the third and fourth grades together, before she went off to private school She's a sweet girl. I wish her the best."

The aunt took up her fork and speared a lettuce leaf. "That's what I mean about you being sweet. When I think of the way you've had to give up just about everything you wanted — Frank running out on you, and that job you got fired from, and having to live with me and put up with my ways —"

"That's not the worst of it," the girl said.

The aunt skipped over that. "Well, the worst of it, in my eyes at least, is that somebody like Miss Apple Mason can get the whole world handed to her on a silver platter. That's what I can't stand."

Billy leaned towards them. "She's going to have just as hard a time as anybody else, maybe harder," he said. "You needn't worry."

"Well!" the older woman gasped.

"Eavesdropper," the girl said, smiling.

"I'm a concerned party," he said, and turned back to his coffee, enjoying their silence against his back.

He was not angry. He felt closer to the older woman in her undisguised bitterness than he felt to most people. After all, she was right. The world was grossly unfair, and there was no way around it and no way to tolerate it. He had known that from the first time he had noticed his mother's large, work-worn hands. It was not fair that she had had to labor all her life to support herself and her two children in the style to which she wanted them to become accustomed. Yet it was equally clear to Billy that the whole question of fairness and unfairness was irrelevant. The only thing that mattered was making the best of what you were handed. He was being handed a good deal — because of luck, and his own effort — yet it all might come to nothing. If he mismanaged Apple, he knew, the marriage would be over in a year, his job at an end, and he would find himself back on his mother's doorstep. There was no guarantee.

The thought of the challenge which faced him restored him to good humor. He dumped milk and sugar into his coffee and drank it greedily. In a few more minutes, his future family would be upon him and he would become absorbed in their conversation.

All right, he thought. Let it come. Let them come.

A movement caught his eye, and he looked up to see Mr. Mason — Ham — standing in the door. As he searched the crowded room, his face wore a look of uncertainty as though all his plans, too, hung in the balance; as though his future son-in-law had failed to follow directions, the table had not been saved, the lunch would not be shared, and the day would collapse.

Billy stood up and waved. Ham. How difficult it was to become used to the nickname.

Smiling with relief, Ham made his way across the cafeteria. Billy remained standing. Behind him, the two women turned and stared. Billy was no longer aware of them. Instead he was looking at the face approaching him, at the smile of tremulous gratitude, of amazing surprise. He reached out to grasp the older man's hand, to draw him down into a chair. He had never felt the tremor in that hand before, the forward echo of approaching age.

174

"They were out of the spray!" Mr. Mason cried. "Just dead out of Blue Grass spray!"

"Why, that's too bad, Ham. Surely you can find something —"

"No, no, no!" Ham said, shaking his head. "I've always given her that, every birthday, every Christmas. What else would I get?" Then he looked at Billy hopefully. "You think maybe you could suggest something else? Something around ten dollars?"

"Yes," Billy said. He gave Ham the menu, then glanced at the watching women with a smile. "Apple likes that toilet water, Spring Green. It's ten-fifty in the atomizer. I bet that would do the trick."

"Apple likes that?"

"Wears it every day, even mucking out stalls."

Ham nodded. "I expect that would do. Yes, I expect it would."

"I can pick some up for you after lunch. Have it wrapped and delivered."

"Could you do that?"

Billy was surprised by Ham's surprise. "Sure!"

"Why, thank you," Ham said, staring at the menu as though to hide something in his expression — fear, bewilderment, gratitude, Billy couldn't begin to guess.

"What about the cheeseburger?" Billy suggested after a minute had passed. "That's what I'm going to order for Apple."

Ham laid aside the menu. "That'll be fine, that'll do for me, as well, and I think you might order the same thing for Adeline."

175

Billy smiled as he beckoned to the waitress. The smile seemed to crack the fine surface of his face. "Why, you need me, too," he said, under his breath.

Later he remembered that he had not said it out loud, would never say it, probably, in all the years he would know Ham Mason. But the revelation remained. Try to explain it away as he might — rich people never get any help because no one knows they need it, a man alone in a houseful of women, and so forth — he never could drain all the sweetness from it. The bargain they made that day before the cheeseburgers and the ladies arrived would never need words or signatures on long sheets of legal paper. "Why, you need me, too," Billy would say to himself now and then in the long years to come. That would seem to be enough.

CHAPTER TWELVE

$\mathcal{A}$UNT POLLY was bewildered. Apple and her father were nearly at the altar, yet the wedding wasn't happening; she could tell that from Ham's back. He was as rigid as though he expected an attack from the side where the bridegroom hadn't appeared. An attack, from that direction! There Ham stood in his morning coat with Apple, all frilly on his arm, and the line of his shoulders told Aunt Polly, in the front pew with Adeline, that nothing was happening because the bridegroom, that Billy, hadn't appeared.

Then he came hurtling in from the side door with the best man shuttling after him, finger in vest pocket to check the ring, and Aunt Polly wanted to sigh out her relief and nudge Adeline. She did neither. Another glance at Ham's shoulders told her the situation hadn't improved; she'd misplaced the direction of the attack. Ham was fearing something from behind, something from the great crowd in the white-walled church, all gathered there, as far as Aunt Polly knew, to smile and celebrate.

She craned back to see who was there, but all she could see were Adeline and Ham's friends and a few of Apple's — she wouldn't have recognized Billy's — gazing all glaze-eyed at the altar. The only person she didn't see was Cory; she'd been late getting into her dress and would come flying in long after the other bridesmaids in their picture hats were settled on either side of that pair, the bride and groom.

Ham was handing Apple over now in tune with whatever Reverend Tolbert was saying; Polly had heard those lines so many times she didn't listen. Sometimes she thought the most distinctive thing about the town was that everybody was always still marrying.

Ham turned around and headed towards their pew, and Polly moved her knees to let him climb over and sit next to his wife. As he passed, he gave her a glance: something was wrong, something was still not happening. She guessed it had to do with Cory, his darling, and whatever her lateness meant.

She wanted to poke him, hiss a question, but Adeline was attracting his attention, blowing her nose already into the lace handkerchief she was clutching in her gloved hand. Adeline, of all people, to cry at a wedding! Then Polly remembered Adeline's fear that neither of her daughters would make it to That State of Grace, which was what she called matrimony. Polly had heard her gasping out those fears one evening in her flower garden.

She looked at the altar. The two of them, the young couple, were alone now, hand in hand in front of the minister, who would have given them his standard speech the afternoon before, about patience and putting the cap back on the toothpaste — as good advice as any, as far as Polly knew. His talk would have followed in tone and content the lecture Apple was given, alone, by Dr. Brown to go with the round blue plastic box that contained her diaphragm. Polly knew there was no way to smooth their path, and fools who pretended to help usually only made matters worse; Apple and that Billy would learn soon enough, a rainy day at Delray Beach would be their first lesson.

She remembered her own first time with Pickle; how he had fumbled and fussed until, out of a charitable impulse, she'd reached out and put his thing in herself. She glanced at Ham to close off that train of thought.

He was looking at her, and Polly realized she hadn't seen him so agitated since they were both children, hiding in the attic on Locust Road, afraid of what was coming next.

"What's wrong?" she whispered, leaning across Adeline to touch his arm, and just at that moment, she saw Ham twist his head towards the altar and realized that it was happening — the vows were being exchanged. Something essential was no longer missing.

It was Corinne.

There she stood, next to Apple, as though she'd sprung from nowhere — all those bridesmaids parting like the Red Sea to let her through.

Corinne reached out to take Apple's bouquet — it was time for the ring — the organ roared in its loft and the minister was about to start the I do's.

Wonder of wonders, Polly thought. Miracle of miracles, and she whispered to Adeline, "How did Frankie get that dress finished in time?"

Adeline put her finger to her lips, but Ham turned and showed relief and gratitude standing out like extra features on his face. "We didn't know till the last minute if she'd do it!"

"Hush," Adeline said.

Polly studied Corinne. She had always been her favorite of the two girls. She was handsome; they were two of a kind in that. Handsome would last, Polly knew, from her own experience. And she had energy. Apple would say what was on her mind and other people's, but Corinne would up and do.

Polly liked her new haircut — certainly done in New York — with twisty curls down the sides and a short brush in back; even that ridiculous picture hat couldn't make her look pastel. Frankie had cut the bodice of Corinne's dress down in the back, and Polly admired her niece's broad shoulders, made not to carry burdens but to sprout wings. Oh yes, she had excessive dreams for Cory! She had watched her all her life.

Frankie had cut the waist of the dress too tight, though. It was splitting open in the back.

Adeline noticed at the same time; she shook her head irritably, as though dislodging a fly. Everything else was perfect — the masses of white roses and red poppies, the candles gleaming, the smilax heaped on the altar — but there was Cory with her dress split open in the back and nothing Polly could see underneath except skin.

It wasn't like Frankie to misestimate. She was in the back of the church, watching; she'd be wild when she saw it.

The eyes of the whole congregation seemed to fasten on

that oblong of bare skin. It was only an inch or two long and perhaps two inches wide, and it would have passed unnoticed on most occasions. This was a perfect occasion, though, Polly thought — weather, clothes, flowers, expectations — so that piece of skin was a slap in the face, almost an indecency.

"Nobody's going to notice," Polly whispered to Adeline.

"How Frankie could —" Adeline began, then covered her mouth with her hand. The minister was asking if anyone had objections to the marriage.

Polly held an old grudge against ministers for stopping after that question, sometimes for minutes together while they combed the congregation, looking for trouble. Reverend Tolbert like all his kind stopped and looked the crowd up and down, waiting for someone to speak.

And Corinne did.

Her voice floated over the heads of the little group at the altar. "Apple can't marry this man."

Polly wondered why she didn't just call him by his name. Billy looked about thirteen years old, scared stiff, jerking around and staring. Apple kept her eyes on the minister.

There was a rustle, a sigh, a quick rush of whispers, soon hushed, and then the congregation gathered itself to face trouble. Polly had felt that before — a group massing and turning to face the intruder, like cattle when a dog runs into the field.

She looked at Ham. He was pursing his mouth, drawing up words, but there was nothing to say. Cory had the floor.

The minister, having brought this trouble on them, bobbed and smiled at Cory as though she'd made a remark about the weather. He tried to go on — they were at the crucial part. "Dearly beloved —"

"Apple doesn't love him and he doesn't love her," Corinne insisted, turning to face the audience. They were an audience now, Polly thought. Next there would be applause, or boos.

She heard the comments beginning behind her — "That girl, always causing trouble." "Really unforgivable!" "Poor Adeline!" She put her face in her hands.

Ham was scrambling to get out of the pew.

The organist, dear old Dr. Folk, plunged into a full-horn version of "Onward, Christian Soldiers." Ham gave Polly a tormented look, and she remembered he'd chosen that hymn to be played at his funeral. He sank back into his seat as though felled.

Nobody could speak through the trumpeting of the organ. The minister stood gaping like a fish. Billy's back was set against the audience, and Apple was reaching for her sister. Her veil hid her profile, but Polly knew she was smiling. Oh the mischief in those two — the one who said it, the other who did it! No one would break them apart.

As for Corinne, she was still facing the audience, looking as though she'd seen a vision, when Apple's little hand slid along her arm and turned her towards the altar.

And then, just as the tension had to break — they couldn't stand there paralyzed through all the verses of "Onward" — Frankie came flying down the aisle. She had on her Sunday dress, but she carried her workday purse, full, Polly knew, of remedies for all occasions.

Frankie is in her element, Polly thought.

182

Ham sighed when Frankie flew by, and Adeline took her hands down from her face.

Frankie grabbed hold of the back of Corinne's dress and jerked that white space out of existence. Then she dropped to her knees. Pins were in her mouth before Polly saw her put them there; without letting go of Cory's dress, Frankie reached for one and jabbed it in.

It took all of a minute to pin that hole up. Meanwhile the organ went on roaring and everybody stayed in their places. Polly saw that poor Billy turn and look at Apple as though he was drowning, and Apple reached for his hand. Her other hand, her left, was holding on to Cory.

Dear old Dr. Folk must have been watching in his mirror, because as soon as the dress was pinned up, he brought the organ to a shuddering halt. In the silence the organ huffed and wrangled with itself, and the audience began to shift and peep, coming out of its trance.

Frankie stood up and ran back down the aisle without looking at anybody.

The minister took a deep breath and began, "Dearly beloved," and in less than five minutes Apple and Billy were kissing.

Aunt Polly looked around and saw Billy's mother and sister, right across the aisle, alone in the front pew on the groom's side; they were crying and they both had handkerchiefs. She remembered that the sister had been meant to be matron of honor and had bowed out without even one complaint when Apple told her to: Cory was home, Cory had to have the dress, the role, the occasion. Well, Aunt Polly thought, that girl, that sister, at least knows what to expect out of life — eternal replacements. No one is essential. It looked to her as though the mother had learned the same lesson.

The organ shouted then like a beast of prey turned loose, and everyone surged down the aisle, after Apple in her white whirls and Billy, his back as solemn as a totem pole. Polly didn't see where Cory went.

Later she found her, drinking champagne and eating crabmeat, a big lump of it, with her fingers. She was sitting on the terrace wall, and the crowd in the tent behind her seemed to have faded out of her awareness.

"Good crabmeat," she said when Polly came up. "You had any?" She took another gulp of champagne.

"Young lady, I did not hunt you down to discuss crabmeat," Polly said, sitting down beside her on the low wall.

"Now don't begin!"

"I have to! Your parents are never going to be able to bring themselves to say a word, and Apple and Billy will be leaving in no time at all for Delray" — Corinne made a face — "and it just goes against my grain to let you get away with this behavior."

"I already got away with it, Aunt Polly. You were there," Corinne said. "Have some crabmeat."

Polly absorbed that a moment. "The way you busted out of that dress, I think you ought to put yourself on a diet," Polly grumbled, knowing she had lost. She had a dozen things to say, but they had all deserted her. She remembered when she'd stood at that same altar with Pickle, all those years before, her lips as numb as her heart; what if someone had shouted something then? What if someone had stepped forward and told the truth?

But it wasn't the truth, she thought, at least as far as I know, and so she said what she'd been taught to say so many years ago — "You ought to be ashamed" — but her heart wasn't in it.

"They don't love each other the way they ought to," Cory said.

"Who are you to judge, Miss? After the mess you've made —"

"But I know how it ought to be now, and I couldn't bear for Apple —"

"Apple will be fine. She knows what she wants, and I think that Billy knows what he wants, too."

"He and Daddy are as thick as thieves." Cory stood up and stretched till her dress seams creaked. "Those pins are sticking in my back. Apple's going to call me from Delray," she added.

Polly stared at her, wondering, What next? "How come Frankie cut it so tight?"

"I held my stomach in, I still can," Cory said.

Polly put her hand over her mouth as though she was going to laugh or cry — she didn't know which — and then she reached up to grab her. But Cory was already on the wall, walking along in her high heels, balancing with her arms spread out. She was walking along that wall over the Ohio River, skipping now, her skirt tucked up, those pins shooting out of the back of her dress, with a twenty-foot drop on one side and five hundred people a yard away in a yellow-and-white-striped tent.

"Come back here!" Polly called.

"Too late!" Cory called back over her shoulder, and Polly saw that dress ripping open again, all the way up her back.

She stood clenching her hands, watching Cory dart along the wall, her feet hardly touching the bricks. As she cavorted, Polly knew what was happening on this day of days, in the heat and sun, on this particular patch of earth over the Ohio River. Cory might be pregnant, but one thing was sure: she was dancing, dancing on the edge of a twenty-foot drop with all the people she'd ever known inside a tent a yard away.

And she was loving it.